LAST
RITE

STEPHEN PENNER

ISBN-13: 978-0615865737
ISBN-10: 0615865739

Last Rite (Maggie Devereaux Mystery #3)

Cover image by richsouthwales. Cover design by Stephen Penner.

LAST
RITE

1. Rude Awakening

Her name was Maggie Devereaux.

She had the worst headache of her life.

And something smelled awful.

Those were the only things she was sure of as the fog blanketing her mind began to recede. She opened one eye. The light stabbed into her brain like a saber. She squinted against the pain and tried to recognize her surroundings.

She had no idea where she was, not specifically. Generally, though, she was reasonably certain she was in a hotel room. The ugly, patterned bed cover and the nondescript watercolor prints on the wall confirmed that.

Forcing open the other eye, she stared up at the white stucco ceiling. There was no way she was going to try sitting up. Not yet. Not if she didn't want her stomach to eject itself through her nose.

She rolled her head to the side to catch a glimpse out of the window whose existence was suggested by the light coming from that side of the room. Sheer drapes blocked the details of the view, but her eyes rested on something else anyway.

The note on the pillow next to her.

She started to prop herself up onto one arm, but decided against it as her brain threatened to explode through her skull.

Instead, thick clumsy fingers grappled with the paper, then raised it toward the ceiling so she could read it safely from her necessarily prone position.

> *Maggie,*
>
> *1. I don't know where the Book is either.*
>
> *2. You didn't do it.*
>
> *3. Neither did I.*
>
> *-Sinclair*

Maggie closed her eyes again and tried to will away the throbbing between her temples. It didn't work.

Book. What book? She liked books.

Sinclair. She knew a Sinclair, didn't she? Sinclair Lewis? That sounded familiar. He wrote a book, right?

Images started to float through her mind. A blond man with a goatee and a scar on his cheek. He was handsome. A dark-haired man with bright blue eyes. He was even more handsome. An older couple in a shop. A police-woman. A baby. Two babies. A castle. A university. A book.

The Book!

She sat straight up in the bed.

"Arrrgh!" She doubled over again into a fetal position. The pain radiated down her spinal cord and into every nerve of her body.

What had she done to herself that made her entire body hurt from the inside out?

The agony subsided enough for her to recall her last thought: the Book. Her Book. The Dark Book of Rites and Damnation. Instinctively, her hand reached out for the tome. Part of her knew it wouldn't be there, but she still wasn't firing on all cylinders, and she usually kept the book close at hand. She remembered that much, although she was having trouble remembering why. So when her hand confirmed the ancient book wasn't lying next to her atop the hotel bed, she wasn't sure where else it might be.

'I don't know where the Book is either.'

She opened her eyes—slowly—and surveyed the room again. She had to get up. The Book was missing. She didn't know where it was, and neither did Sinclair, whoever he was. Who was Sinclair? Not Sinclair Lewis. Not an author. But something about books? A librarian? No. And did he know about the Book too? She thought no one knew.

No, someone else knew. Someone knew about the Book. Or the magic.

Magic? There's no such thing as magic. Her own mother had told her that once.

Maggie closed her eyes again and took in a deep breath. She was lost, in pain, and confused. Handsome blond man knew about her book. Someone else knew about her magic. And she didn't even know what magic he knew about.

It was a "he." *He* knew about the magic.

The cuter guy. The dark-haired one with the blue eyes and the sparkling smile.

Iain.

Iain!

And then the memories came flooding back, every one of them a hot poker in her brain, setting fire to her synapses. Her mother's death. Her grandmother's death. Going to Scotland.

Meeting Iain.

Studying under Professor Macintyre. Meeting Kelly Anderson. The murders. Sergeant Warwick. Inspector Cameron.

Devan Sinclair.

The kidnapped baby. The trip to Wales. The trip to Ireland.

The castle. Sarah MacKenzie.

The Dark Book.

The magic.

Iain.

"Oh, Iain," she moaned. The last clear memory she had was of Iain walking away from her, ignoring her tears, ignoring his name as she called after him. Walking away from her. Forever.

That memory hurt more than the spikes in her skull and she finally managed to pull herself into a sitting position. She lowered her head into her hands and tried to remember where she was. But it was no use. Her last memory was of Iain walking away beneath the castle in Visegrád. So, she must be in Hungary.

She raised her head and looked toward the nightstand. There was definitely a telephone and some hotel stationery there. She also definitely couldn't read it from that distance without her glasses that were also resting atop the nightstand. A tender scoot and an outstretched hand later she was pulling her glasses on and tucking her thick auburn hair behind her ears. She picked up the small notepad next to the phone.

'Hotel Regency. Edinburgh.'

Edinburgh. Of course.

She lowered her head into her hands again. She had absolutely no memory of travelling back to Scotland, and certainly not to Edinburgh.

Why was she in Edinburgh?

How had she gotten there?

How long had she been there?

And really, what was that horrible smell?

The pain in her head, and the accompanying nausea, seemed to be subsiding as she remembered things. But try as she might, she couldn't recall how she'd ended up in a hotel room in Edinburgh.

That bit of amnesia remained, and with it a dull throbbing in her head and a tender uneasiness in her gut. Still, she felt better enough that she thought she could make it to the bathroom. Some water on her face and a cool washcloth on her neck sounded like just the ticket. Besides, she really had to pee.

Maggie stood up gingerly and extended a hand to the wall. One eye open, she slowly felt her way to the bathroom. As she approached, at least she thought she knew what the smell was. Along with everything else she'd forgotten, she must have forgotten to flush. She flicked on the bathroom light.

"Ahhhhhhh!" Her own scream split her aching head right down the middle.

But she didn't care about the pain.

She only cared about the blood-soaked dead man in the bathtub. And the subsequent pounding on the door.

"Police! Open up!"

2. Keeping Up Disappearances

"Aw, crap," Maggie said as the adrenaline dumped into her bloodstream.

She knew she needed to get away from the cops. It didn't even occur to her to open the door and tell the truth. Dead man in bathtub plus police at door equals climb out the window.

The knocking became louder and she heard them fiddling with the door handle. She looked at the man in the tub. She didn't recognize him, although she wasn't sure she would have anyway through all the blood. Still, there was something familiar about the scene.

She reached into her pocket and pulled out her cell phone. She stared at it for a moment. It was a new model; she didn't remember upgrading. But it only took a minute to find the camera app. She snapped a quick picture of the scene, then returned the phone to her pocket.

She tried to run back to the bed, but her headache prevented it. Instead, she walked quickly, pulled her backpack from the floor and crossed to the window, scooping up the note from Sinclair along the way.

She could hear the door unlocking as she opened the window. Looking out, she discovered she was on the second floor.

It was too far to jump, but she was out of time. The hotel room door was opening.

"We're coming in!" they shouted.

"And I'm heading out," she whispered to herself.

She turned herself around and backed out of the window, holding onto the sill. She lowered herself as far as far as she could, then let go just as the police burst into the room.

She dropped to the pavement below with a painful shock to her ankles. She actually crumpled to the concrete alleyway and fell onto her backpack. For the first time since she'd regained her senses, she was glad she didn't have the Dark Book. Landing on that would have hurt.

She sat for a moment and rubbed her ankles. Her mind raced as she imagined what the police would think when they found the body. Her heart raced as she wondered whether she'd be able to walk again before they realized she went out the window.

Then she remembered something.

She didn't need to jump. She could have used the magic to lower herself safely. She remembered the first spell she ever cast: *Mhaidhid inh chuimriachan anh-i chonrig riátsha cho inh Thalum.* Its translation: 'Tear asunder the bonds which chain this object to the Earth.' That might have been a good thing to remember before jumping out of a second story window.

Then she rubbed her sore ankles and remembered something else.

There was no healing spell.

Even though her magic-wielding ancestor, Brìghde Innes, was called a 'healer' back in 1620.

The mental assault of bits and pieces of disjointed information was disorienting. She didn't know what she knew or why it mattered. Her head was starting to hurt again, nearly as much as her ankles. So she was almost relieved to be distracted from her fractured thoughts by the old woman who started yelling at her. Unfortunately, she couldn't understand a thing the woman was saying through her thick Scottish brogue.

"Wutteryoo doonthar?!" the heavy set, gray-mopped lady shouted as she plodded over, her fat fist shaking in the air. "Yeel be bluckintha wayuh."

Maggie blinked at the woman. She wished she had some way of just snapping her fingers and understanding her.

"I'm sorry," Maggie replied. "I didn't understand what you said."

The woman huffed and shoved her meaty hands onto her hips. "Aye sayud, yoor bluckin tha wayuh. The trooksill no beyabuhl ta mayk tha duhlivrees."

Maggie stared at the woman's mouth as she spoke, hoping that might help her understand. She thought she got the last word. "Deliveries?"

"Aye, duhlivrees!" The woman cast her arms about at the loading dock behind the hotel. "Thayll be heyuh annee moomunt."

"Deliveries," Maggie repeated. She pulled herself painfully to her feet. Her ankles were going to be sore for a while. "Going to be here any moment."

"Aye," the lady huffed. "Annee moomunt."

Maggie was about to ask for those few moments more, when she heard distant sirens approaching. It was time to leave.

"Right then, well, thank you," she said. "No hard feelings and all that."

The woman offered a reluctant smile then reached out and grabbed Maggie's arm with surprising force. "Canaydiyun, then, are ye?"

Maggie thought for a moment, then smiled back. "Yes. Yes,

I'm Canadian."

The woman let go just as the back door of the hotel opened and out stepped two policemen. Maggie hitched her backpack higher and hurried away on stinging ankles, hopeful that the old lady would steer the police to be on the look-out for a Canadian woman with glasses and a funny walk.

* * *

"Canadian, eh?"

Sergeant Tomkins nodded his head. "Aye, ma'am. We extracted his wallet from his pants pocket. He has a driver's license from British Columbia. It lists his address as Vancouver. We checked with the front desk. They said he wasn't a guest here."

Inspector Lindsey Benson tapped her lips as she visually examined the bloody carcass in the bath tub. The forensics officers were still photographing the scene and marking potential evidence for collection. "Had they any idea what he was doing here?"

"Here, in this room?" Tomkins clarified, "Or here, in Edinburgh."

Benson pursed her lips and shrugged. "Either, I suppose."

"No, ma'am," answered Tomkins. "Neither."

Benson looked down at him and frowned. She was a tall woman, six feet in heels, with fine blond hair pulled into a loose bun at the base of her neck. Tomkins was a bit on the short side and drank a little too much to keep his gut trim. He smiled at his superior. "But I knew to ask about both."

Benson smiled. She had a lopsided smile that was creasing a wrinkle on her right cheek, to go along with the beginnings of the crow's-feet at the corners of her eyes. At least the knee-length skirts hid the varicose veins. Damn getting older as a woman. Men had no idea.

"Good job, then," she said. "And follow up. I want to know

why he was in Edinburgh, and why he was in this room."

She tapped her lips again, only partly to wave away the smell of blood and feces filling the small bathroom.

"Who was this room rented to?"

Tomkins pulled out his notepad. "Eh... The girl at the front desk said it was a bloke name of Sinclair. Devan Sinclair."

* * *

"Sinclair," Maggie muttered as she examined the note again. "What was he doing in Edinburgh?"

She stopped in the middle of the sidewalk and looked around the neighborhood she found herself in, the rows of slate-roofed townhomes snaking along the street toward the shops at the next busy intersection.

"What am *I* doing here?"

She shook her head and looked down at the note. Sinclair knew about the Dark Book. And he must have known about the dead man in the bathtub. What else could he have meant by 'I didn't do it'? But then, why would he just leave her there with a dead body in the next room?

Then she remembered her phone. Or rather, that she had taken a picture with her phone. She pulled it from her pocket and quickly navigated to the photo gallery. A swipe and screen-pinch later and the photo of the dead man filled the screen.

She saw it immediately. And she was afraid she knew what it meant.

* * *

"Hey, I hadn't noticed that before." Tomkins pointed at the dead man's face. "What do you suppose that means?"

Benson leaned down as the last photographs were taken and the forensics officers retreated into the main part of the hotel room. She examined the corpse's face, crusted red and black with blood.

"Is that...?" she started.

"A stone," Tomkins finished. "Across the bridge of his nose."

Benson frowned. "Well, it must mean something. I'm just not sure what. It is damn odd, though."

"That's not the only thing that's odd," said the tall brunette woman who had slipped into the bathroom to stand over the body. "This whole scene looks staged somehow. The body is just...wrong."

Forensic Investigator Emma Valentine rested her chin on her fist. "Unless," she continued, "he had some sort of degenerative disease or something."

"Nice to see you, Emma," Murdock greeted the new arrival. "I'm unaware of the man's medical history yet."

"No need for it," Valentine said with a crooked smile. She pushed up her sleeve and pulled on a thick, blue latex glove. "I've got a pretty specific hunch."

"About what?" Tomkins asked.

"His legs are too long," Valentine replied, not obviously on point. "And so are his arms."

"For what?" Benson asked.

"For his torso," Valentine answered. "Which means, either, he had some disease, or..."

She knelt down and braced herself against the side of the bathtub. Then she slid her gloved hand under the grisly remains. She probed under the body, animating it into a marionette-like dance. After a moment, she extracted her glove—its blue well hidden by the blackish blood hanging from it in half-coagulated strands.

"Nope, I was right," she announced.

"About what?" Benson asked, scanning the body visually

but declining to replicate Valentine's examination.

"It's gone," Valentine said.

"What is?" Benson asked.

"His spine," Valentine answered. "That's why his ribs are resting on his pelvis. The autopsy will confirm it, but whoever did this, for whatever reason, they removed all of his lumbar vertebrae."

Benson nodded. "We'll need to figure out that reason then. And I'd wager it's the same reason they set a stone across his eyes."

Valentine leaned over and stared down at the bloody rock. After a moment, she stood up straight and said, "Well, now, that's just crazy."

* * *

"I must be going crazy," Maggie whispered. "The stone. The same type of stone. It's happening again."

She stared at the photo for several more moments, then looked up and around at the Scottish capital. A lone, straggling police car made its hurried way toward her hotel room, not bothering with lights any more. She slipped her phone away and considered her situation.

"Why am I in Edinburgh?" she asked herself.

Then another question. "Why was Sinclair here?"

More thought, then, "Who was that dead guy in the bathtub?"

And finally, as she began fiddling with the necklace she always wore around her neck, only to result in her hand tracing the empty chain frantically and her heart dropping at the thought of the police scouring the murder scene in the hotel room she'd just vacated:

"Where's my pendant?"

3. Terror on the Highland Express

There was no express train from Edinburgh to Aberdeen. Maggie knew that spelled trouble. If it had been a longer trip, she could have rented a sleeping car and gotten a good night's rest. If it had been a high-speed train, the trip would have been about an hour and she could have forced herself to stay awake. But a three hour train ride, rolling lazily through the Scottish hills? She knew there was no way she would be able to stay awake.

She was exhausted, although she didn't know why. She had awakened in a strange room from a dreamless sleep. She was so curious about the waking up in a strange room part, she forgot to be grateful for the dreamless part.

She was about to remember.

"Tickets, please." The conductor slid open the door to her compartment. There were no other passengers with her. She handed her ticket to the man as the train began pulling away from the station.

He punched her ticket and handed it back to her. "Enjoy your trip."

"Thanks," Maggie replied as she stuffed the ticket back into her backpack. She leaned her head against the wall to look out the window. "I will."

But she was wrong.

The sky was a mottled mosaic of gray, its swirling smears of slate and ash filtering the sunlight into a twilight glow. The blotchy patches high above melted into steaks of silver and charcoal that poured down to a circle of dead treetops, their black braches reaching for the half-light with gnarled fingers. Within the circle of trees was a concentric ring of weathered gravestones, the remains of the ruined cemetery, in the middle of which stood a bewildered and befuddled Maggie.

She turned slowly around, appraising and counting the headstones. Thirteen. Each one bleached white and facing the center of the circle. Facing her.

She walked forward to the oldest-looking grave marker. The whitest, thinnest, most worn. A flat, smooth testament to a life lost to the past.

The words carved into the stone were too worn away. She couldn't read the name. She reached out to feel where the words once were. Where they still were—just barely. But her fingertips were a poor substitute for her eyes and she couldn't decipher the shallow grooves by touch alone.

She looked down at the journal in her left hand. She opened it. It was blank. She tore out the first page and laid it atop the remnants of the letters on the gravestone. Using the pencil in her right hand, she made a rubbing of the inscription. The nearly forgotten name slowly materialized onto the torn page from Maggie's book.

B R I D G E T

"Bridget?" Maggie asked aloud.

In response, a voice drifted across the wind, "Don't you remember?"

She spun around. But there was no one there. She was alone.

She looked down again at the sheet of paper in her hand. The white block letters within gray pencil lead had been replaced by black ink, written in a strong and foreign hand:

Brìghde

Maggie stared at the name for several moments. A chill swelled through the air. She turned her attention to the next headstone.

Again it was too weathered to read. Again she traced her fingers over the letters. This time she recognized the familiar letters:

M A R G A R E T

She stood up and noticed for the first time that a waist-high iron fence surrounded this grave, separating it from the others.

"Why is this here?" she asked.

The cold air answered, "Don't you remember?"

The iron gate at the foot of the grave swung in the growing wind. It clanked arhythmically against the fence. Maggie stepped out and proceeded to the next grave.

She circumnavigated the graveyard, examining each headstone. Each time she was able to discern a name. Each time she failed to recognize it. Each time, the wind asked her, "Don't you remember?"

The sky was growing darker, the day colder. A light rain began to fall. Not enough to take shelter from, but it clung to her cheeks as she reached the eleventh gravestone.

This one was different. Not bleached into colorlessness, not completely anyway. It held a golden hue, with faint purple veins spreading vibrantly through the stone. When she touched it, the stone held warmth. The name was clear as day, its golden paint still visible inside the chiseled letters:

K A T E

She stared at the name. She knew she knew. Or at least, she knew she should know. But she couldn't find a candle to light the memory.

The voice was equally familiar. It came not from the air itself, but from directly behind her, as if the woman were standing not a foot away. And it was tinged with sadness. "Don't you remember?" she asked.

Maggie turned, but there was no one there. She turned back and stared at the gravestone. Like the others, she didn't remember. Unlike the others, it filled her with shame.

Tears spilling from silent eyes, she stepped to the next headstone.

ELLEN

The tears were joined by a muffled sob and Maggie dropped to her knees before the cold stone. She waited for the question, but it never came. There was no point to it. Maggie knew the name, but didn't remember the person. She had been too young to remember.

The rain trickled down her neck as she kneeled, head bowed, before her mother's grave. The wind blew her damp hair against her face. The chill was seeping into her bones. She pushed up off the muddy ground and stepped to the next grave.

The last grave.

Her grave.

MAGGIE

Her name was clear, even through the growing gloom She stepped forward, unbelieving, to feel the letters, as if the very vibrancy of her touch might wash them away. But before her fingers could reach the stone, the ground began to loosen and give way beneath her feet. She scrambled backward, but the earth caved in and she had to leap to the side to avoid being drawn into the open grave that appeared before her when the cloud of dust and dirt settled.

Maggie kept her feet firmly atop Brìghde Innes' grave and craned her neck to peer into her own. It was deep and dark and exactly her size. She looked again at the head stone.

MAGGIE

"But I'm not dead," she protested.

This time, the response came not over the air, but through the ground, gravelly and dark. A skeletal hand shot up through the soil beneath her feet and seized her ankle.

"DON'T... YOU... REMEMBER?!"

Panicked, Maggie wrenched her leg away and stumbled toward the center of the circle as the full corpse—rotten and mummified—pushed itself out of the grave. Maggie watched in growing horror as body after body clawed its way out of grave after grave.

She retreated slowly from the advancing circle of the reanimated corpses of her ancestors. Unsure where to run, she found small hope when she bumped into the large tree which suddenly stood in the middle of the grave circle.

She climbed.

The bark was cold and slimy. Her feet slipped against the knotted trunk as she reached for the lowest branch. Her hands grasped the clammy wood and she pulled herself up just as the corpses reached the tree.

She dropped her journal as she climbed higher.

The zombies could claw at the tree but their rotten muscles lacked the strength to pull themselves up the branches. She was safe.

Or not.

"Don't you remember?" they moaned as they began to rock the tree against its moorings.

Maggie climbed higher, as high as she could, to the very top, where the black branches barely supported her weight. There were no leaves. No blossoms. No fruit, save a single apple, hanging from the uppermost branch. Twelve reanimated corpses pushed and pulled her tree into a sickening sway. The apple swung before her face like a hypnotist's watch.

She reached out and wrapped her hand around the plump fruit. She plucked it.

"Don't you remember!" the zombies shouted. Not a question—a command. "Don't you *dare* remember!"

The apple crumbled to dust in her palm. It ran through her grasping fingers like so much sand, just as the roots finally gave way and her tree toppled forward, spilling her headlong into the black abyss of her own grave.

"Ahhhhh!!"

She jerked awake and looked around, her heart beating out of her chest. She was still in the train compartment. No grave. That was good.

Mercifully, no one had joined her in the compartment while she was sleeping. She wiped the sweat from her brow and waited for her heart to slow.

It was the first time she'd slept since waking up in the hotel room. In addition to everything else she'd forgotten, she'd also forgotten about the dreams.

She leaned her head against the cool glass of the train window.

At least she knew one thing: she'd used the magic. The nightmares always came after she used the magic.

She just didn't know what she'd done. Or why.

She closed her eyes and concentrated on the calming sway of

the train over the tracks. She wondered how long until Aberdeen. But, in a way, it didn't matter.

She sure as Hell wasn't going back to sleep.

4. Nightmares Come True Too

Ellie MacGregor sat on the floor of the Aberdeen bus station, her spine knocking against the hard marble wall from her shivering despite the unseasonably warm morning. The floor was dirty, but it had been a long time since she cared about getting dirty, since she even noticed dirt. The filth she had seen in her life was well beyond a layer of dust and soot and spilled drinks on a bus station floor.

She was back in Aberdeen. Not out of choice, exactly. Not out of necessity, either. Just because. Because salmon and elephants and people went back to where they came from when it was time to give up and die.

She didn't have anywhere to go. Home hadn't been home since she'd run away two decades ago. When word had reached her that her mom had died, she'd cried. When she'd gotten word her dad had died, she'd celebrated. At least he'd never hurt anyone again. Not her. Not her brothers or sisters either. Not that any of them ever helped her. She didn't want to see them either. They all thought they were better than her because they'd put up with it all and pretended it never happened, but she was too strong to do that.

She looked down at her hands. They weren't very strong hands any more. They were thin and weak and wrinkled well beyond their thirty-some years. She was past the time when she could easily earn the money for her next fix. She could still do it, just not easily.

That left the shelter. She hadn't been in Aberdeen for years, but she knew they had a shelter somewhere. Probably several of them. She wondered where the nearest one was. Then, despite herself, she wondered how far she'd have to go to find that next fix. And where she could go to earn the money for it.

She put her heads in her hands. She would have cried, but she'd forgotten how to let herself do that.

It wasn't getting any better. It never got any better. She was losing what little hope she'd clung to over the years. Maybe the people at the shelter could help her. Maybe if she listened to them this time. Maybe if she followed the rules and asked for help when she was feeling weak. Maybe somebody would actually help her. Maybe someone would at least pretend like they cared.

"Do you need some help, miss?"

Ellie looked up. There was a woman standing over her. A woman with nice clothes and a kind face. A woman a little older than her, but clean and pretty and smiling. A woman like Ellie's mother. Ellie didn't reply. She didn't know what to say. It felt like she didn't even know how to reply.

The woman smiled and crouched down so she was at Ellie's eye level. "I say, do you need some help, miss?"

'Miss.' Ellie liked that. It had been a while since she'd been young enough to warrant a miss. But she wasn't really old enough for a 'ma'am' yet either. She got called lots of things. Most of them weren't very nice. She liked being called 'miss.'

She still felt like she couldn't talk, so she just nodded at the woman with the kind face.

The woman nodded back. "I thought so." She stood up and extended a hand to Ellie. After a moment, Ellie took it—ashamed for the first time in a long time that her hands were dirty—and let the kind woman pull her to her feet.

"You need a place to stay, don't you?" the kind woman asked. "Some food and a bath and somewhere to lay your head while you get back on your feet."

Ellie nodded again. She finally found her voice. "Aye," she croaked.

The kind woman smiled and picked up Ellie's bag for her. Ellie knew it was filthy and stank. The woman pretended it didn't.

"Come with me then," the woman said. "I'll take care of you."

Ellie nodded and started to walk toward the exit with the woman.

"What's your name?" the kind woman asked.

"Ellie," she replied.

The woman smiled but kept her eye on the exit. "Nice to meet you, Ellie. I'm Sarah."

5. Resting Places

Maggie's walk from the train station to her flat had its own dreamlike quality. She knew the way, of course, but it was the times she focused on her journey that she began to get lost. Which street to follow, which way to turn at an intersection, which fork in the winding Aberdeen roads. If she thought about it too hard, she didn't know which way to go. But when she was lost in other thoughts, her feet took her the right way, her subconscious seeming to know that which her conscious mind didn't.

Her memory was still spongy and unreliable. Some things were as clear as day, others as murky as a Highland bog. And there was still that large gap of localized but complete amnesia: she didn't remember a thing between Visegrád and Edinburgh. So it was with a relief similar to waking from a disturbing dream that she turned the final corner and spotted the door to her apartment. She slipped her key into the lock and stepped inside her home for the first time in she didn't know how long—literally.

Her flat was draped in that thick blanket of silence that falls over a residence when its occupant leaves for an extended period. Too short a time to pack up or clean out. But long enough to draw the shades and leave the fridge bare save whatever groceries had been left over at the time of departure. Her trip to Hungary hadn't been entirely impromptu, but it hadn't been long anticipated either. A light dust covered the surfaces. The milk in the fridge had expired.

She walked into her bedroom. The bed was made, the sheets tucked tightly. Her closet doors were closed and her hamper was mostly empty. That same light dust covered everything. Everything except the keyboard of her laptop, tipped open on her desk.

A simple press of the 'on' button confirmed the battery was dead.

She fetched the power cord from her desk drawer and plugged it into the wall, then she turned it on and lay down to rest her spinning head on the fluffed and ready pillow while the computer started up.

* * *

The young man behind the desk didn't look up from his laptop as the police officer entered the small cottage at the entrance to the Aberdeen Municipal Cemetery. Sergeant Elizabeth Warwick was unimpressed by the lack of reception. She had an appointment. She was on time. And she was, after all, the police.

She straightened to her full 5' 9" height and cleared her throat.

"One moment," the young man said. Warwick guessed he was barely twenty. Young enough to not need to shave every day, and immature enough to make that obvious by not doing so that morning. An eager, but inadequate, fuzz dusted his chin and lip, while completely ignoring his cheeks. His red hair was cropped short, but curled nonetheless, and his youthful vanity prevented him from wearing glasses, his need for which was obvious as he squinted at the computer screen only inches from his face. "I just need to update my status."

Warwick rolled her eyes. She knew enough about social

media to know she didn't want to know more.

"Got to go," muttered the young man as he typed, "Coppers just arrived."

He pressed enter and finally looked up at his visitor, his pale blue eyes flashing above his crooked grin. "That ought to get some replies."

Warwick begrudged a curt nod. "I'd imagine." She pulled her coat aside to expose the badge affixed to her belt. "I'm Sergeant Warwick with the Aberdeen Police. I'm here about the grave robbery."

"Right, right." The young man stood up and stepped out from behind his desk. His blue shirt had some sort of stain toward the bottom and his worn khakis bunched atop scuffed brown shoes, dried mud caked to their soles. "Thanks for coming. I'm Douglas Macafie, the night watchman here. Everybody calls me Dougie. I'm the one what discovered the grave this morning."

"Have you pulled the file for the grave, Dougie?" Warwick got right to business. "I'd to like to see whatever information you have regarding the person buried there."

"Er, no," Dougie replied. "I was about to. I just hadn't got to it quite yet is all."

Warwick nodded at the laptop. "Well, first thing's first, eh? Why don't you pull the file and meet me at the grave." She gestured vaguely toward the cemetery sprawling out behind the cabin. "Which way is it?"

Dougie stepped just outside the front door and pointed. "You see that tall oak tree there? Just walk straight for it. The grave is on the right. You'll know it when you see it."

Warwick frowned. "Was it a mausoleum?" She hoped it was a mausoleum.

"No, ma'am." Dougie shook his head. "They dug her right

up, they did."

Warwick thanked the young man and stepped from the cottage. It was a warm afternoon, but a chilling breeze confirmed autumn was at hand. She followed the gravel footpath toward the tree Dougie had pointed out. She did her best to ignore the significance of the graves she passed.

Whistling through the graveyard, she thought with a wry grin. She saw enough death; she didn't need a reminder. Especially not one that gave a peaceful facade to the violence she had seen in her career. There was something artificial about the well-manicured lawn resting genteelly atop the worm-ridden bodies filling the earth beneath her feet. As if someone were concealing the evidence of the one thing we all know is certain, and we all pretend isn't.

The grave was visible as she crested a small hill. Unmistakable. The lush green carpet of grass was torn open, rich black earth spilling out of the wound like so much coagulated blood. The gray headstone was erect and intact, giving testimony to who had been interred there, but unable to stop the monstrous souls who dared uncover what humanity had worked so hard to conceal.

Warwick approached the site cautiously, aware that her very presence impacted the crime scene. Although surely spoiled somewhat by the night watchman, she didn't need to add to the contamination. Careful steps on already trodden grass led her to the gravestone. She crouched down and read the inscription, pretending to ignore the stench from the dank hole at her feet.

JENNIFER N. BURNS
Beloved Mother Daughter and Sister
Born 1861. Died 1917.

Warwick frowned. The name meant nothing to her. Like all the rest in the cemetery, she supposed. But it meant something to someone.

"Quite a bit of work, eh?" Dougie had arrived, marching through the mud and grass without a care. He handed her the file before she gently pushed him away from the grave and behind the headstone. He complied, although with a puzzled expression. "In one night they did that," he went on. "No small task that."

Warwick looked again at the hollowed ground. It was nearly the full six feet deep, not to mention six feet long and two or three feet wide. Nearly one hundred cubic feet of heavy, damp earth. Absolutely back-breaking work.

"How do you know it was more than one person?" she asked.

Dougie rubbed the back of his neck. "Well, I suppose I don't know for sure," he admitted, "but that's a hell of a lot of work for just one man to do overnight, in the dark, with no one noticing. You'd have to be crazy to do that alone. They use heavy equipment to dig the graves now, but even back in the day with shovels, it was a two-man job."

Warwick looked down into the grave again. "Doesn't look big enough for two men."

"No, ma'am," Dougie agreed. "One man dug while the other rested." He patted his young biceps. "Moving earth is hard work."

The coffin was visible at the bottom of the hole. Clumps of moist earth clung to its wooden lid, which was cross-hatched with scars from the grave robbers' shovel-blades. There were a few half-destroyed boot prints visible in the loose dirt atop the casket.

Warwick looked at the date on the gravestone. Miss Burns had been in the ground for nearly a century. Warwick supposed whatever decomposition was needed to take place to render a body skeletonized had long since occurred. She confirmed the coffin had a two-part-lid then stepped around to the foot of the grave.

She gave him the file back and extended an arm. "Can you

give me a hand?"

Dougie offered an unsettling grin. "Are you going in?"

"Well, I can hardly inspect the remains from up here, can I?" Warwick asked.

Dougie nodded, still wide-eyed and grinning, but didn't say anything. He took a hold of Warwick arm and steadied her as she half-jumped onto the casket, careful not to tread on the shoe prints.

"You didn't come down here, did you?" She looked up to regard his shoes, but they were out of sight behind the piles of dirt.

He too looked down toward his shoes. "Er, no, ma'am," he assured rather unconvincingly.

Warwick returned her attention to the business beneath her own feet. The smell was stronger within the grave, the sweetness of fresh dirt mixed with the sickening pungency of death. Taking a deep breath of the foul air, she squatted and grabbed the top half of the coffin lid.

It opened with no resistance. Confirmation that it had last been opened hours—not decades—before, by the grave robbers. Or by a curious Dougie Macafie, Warwick considered. She supposed one had to be at least comfortable around death to work at a cemetery. Dougie seemed beyond comfortable—downright interested.

The smell was predictably strongest inside the confines of the casket. Warwick gagged despite herself, and felt her eyes water as she fought off the urge to vomit. She managed a quick scan of the contents before having to let the lid slam shut and grabbing Dougie's hand to pull herself out of the grave.

She reduced her physiological response to a few dry coughs.

"Was it empty?" Dougie asked with a bit too much interest.

Warwick shook her head as she brushed her hands off on each other. "No. The body is still there. It's a skeleton in half-rotted clothes, but appears mostly undisturbed. Her arms are still crossed across her chest."

Dougie peered into the grave. "Mostly?"

Warwick nodded. "The forensic officers will have to confirm it, but it looked to me like something was missing."

Dougie's eyes widened again. The grin returned. "What?"

Warwick frowned and glanced down at Jennifer Burns' coffin. "Her hand."

* * *

Maggie lifted her hands from the keyboard.

Missing. Gone. Erased.

Everything. Every last email, received or sent or drafted or anything, during the period she was starting to think of as 'The Lost Weeks' was simply gone. Deleted. As if she hadn't existed then.

There wasn't even any spam.

She wasn't the most prolific emailer, but she always got notifications from the university, or notes from friends, or business offers from Nigerian princes. But there was nothing. Everything just stopped after her trip to Hungary. Just like her memory. The similarity was accentuated by the fact that the spam had started up again that morning. She already had one email for cheap prescriptions and another to make 'mi11ion$' from home.

She leaned back and ran her fingers through her thick brown hair.

The computer thought she didn't exist during The Lost Weeks. She wondered if her friends and family agreed.

6. Why Can't You *Be Traist*?

Maggie looked up at the sign hanging above her aunt and uncle's shop:

MAcTARY'S WOOLENS, EST. 1897

Gold letters atop a red plaid, with lines of white, yellow, and light blue criss-crossing the design. The Innes Clan tartan. She recognized it. She *remembered* it.

Well, that's good, she thought.

She turned and reached for the door handle. Her eyes met the brass door knocker. She recognized its design too. A boar's head, the lower tusk extending above the snout, and encircled by a leather strap bearing the words, *Be Traist*, the Innes Clan motto: 'Be True' in Middle Scots.

Not only did she remember the motto, she remembered her grandmother's last words to her: 'As long as you stay true to what's right, I will always be with you.'

So why did she feel so alone just then? There was a hole inside her. One exacerbated by her location, she could tell. But its cause hid in the recesses of her still inadequately lighted memory.

She shook off the feeling and, nodding to the motto—*her* motto—she pushed open the door and walked into the store.

"Maggie!" her aunt shouted as she appeared.

Aunt Lucy was behind the register. She had been a second mother to Maggie since her arrival in Scotland the previous fall, and fully looked the part with her gray-tinged curls and oversized sweater. She dropped the handful of postcards she'd been stuffing into a wire add-on rack and hurried across the cluttered shop.

Maggie felt a wash of relief. Apparently only her computer had forgotten about her.

"Where have you been, lass?" Lucy complained as she crossed the shop and embraced her niece. "We've not heard from you in weeks. We've been worried sick."

Maggie hugged her aunt tightly. The solidness of another human body was welcome relief from the ethereal dissociation she'd felt since awakening in the Edinburgh hotel room.

"I know," Maggie said into her aunt's neck. "I'm sorry. I'm not really sure what's going on either."

Lucy pulled her niece away and held her by the shoulders. "Are you okay, Maggie? What's happened?"

Maggie frowned. She wasn't sure where to begin. Worse yet, she didn't know, literally, where to end.

"I— I'm not sure," She started. "It's complicated."

Lucy's expression softened. An empathic glow lit the corner of her eyes. "Aye, lass. Love is always complicated."

Maggie cocked her head. "Love?"

Before Lucy could reply, her husband Alex burst through the curtains from the storeroom. A large, bearded man, dressed in his usual plaid shirt and one-size-too-small pants, he often spoke before assessing the situation. "I heard the door," he bellowed. "Is Iain here already?"

Lucy shot an angry glare. Maggie felt her heart jump, then sink.

Iain.

Damn.

She'd forgotten. Again. How could she forget Iain? How could she forget how he'd abandoned her beneath the castle, her hands bleeding and her heart breaking? She looked down at her palms. Pink lines crossed over her natural palm-lines. Nearly healed scars. But then, scars never really healed. That's why they were scars.

"Oh, Maggie. It's you," Alex stammered. Then he regained himself. "It's you!"

He hurried over as Lucy let go of Maggie's shoulders. "How are you?" he asked. "Where have you been?"

Maggie grimaced. "It's complicated," she repeated.

"Complicated?" Alex scoffed. "What's complicated about disappearing off the face of the earth for these past weeks? When Iain got back from your jaunt to Hungary of all places and said you'd run off without him, we were worried sick. You ignored our emails, our voicemails, our—"

"Wait." Maggie raised her palm. "Iain said *I* ran out on *him*?"

Lucy raised an eyebrow at Alex; he returned the look and nodded slowly. "Aye," he said. "Well. Perhaps it's better if we don't get in the middle of that. The important thing is that you're home safe, and no worse for wear."

Maggie reflexively rubbed her forehead. She wasn't so sure about the 'no worse for wear' part. She still wasn't looking forward to trying to sleep that night. She was in no hurry to fall into another open grave.

She was about to pump her aunt and uncle for more information about what Iain had said when the door jingled again and in walked the horse's mouth. Or horse's ass. She wasn't sure. But either way, it was Iain.

"Oh," Lucy said upon seeing him.

"Oh," Iain echoed as he stepped in and saw Maggie.

Alex was finally smart enough to keep his mouth shut.

Maggie pushed her fists onto her hips. "Well, hello, Mr. Grant. Long time, no see."

Iain managed a pained grin. "Aye, well." He shifted his weight. He had a way of holding his 6'2" frame, always strong and comfortable regardless of the situation. His thick black hair fell over his blue eyes as he looked down. "I didn't think we had anything left to say."

"Nothing left to say?" Maggie scoffed. "You never said *anything*. You just walked away."

Iain narrowed his eyes at Maggie. He set his jaw. He pursed his lips into a tight knot. Then he turned to Alex. "I've just come for my last check. You said I could pick it up today. Is it ready?"

It took Alex a stunned moment, but he began nodding. "Oh, aye. Aye, Iain. I'll go fetch it." He seemed glad to extricate himself from the situation.

"Perhaps I should go help him," Lucy suggested with a step toward the curtain Alex had already disappeared through.

Iain waved her off. "No need, Lucy. I'll wait outside."

And with that, he slipped out onto the sidewalk.

"Coward," Maggie growled after him. Then she turned to her aunt. "What did he mean, his 'last check'?"

Lucy frowned. "He gave his notice when he got back from your trip."

"His notice?" Maggie repeated. "He quit?"

"Aye, he quit," Alex confirmed as he returned from the back of the store. "The best damned store manager any man ever had, and he's moving to Edinburgh. Whatever happened between you two, I hope it was worth it."

"Edinburgh?" Maggie's heart sank even deeper. It was one thing to have to straighten things out over the next few weeks. She'd always been able to soothe his feelings and bring him around. But how was she supposed to do that if he was a hundred miles away?

She snatched the check out of Alex' hand. "I'll give him his check. And he'll give me some answers."

As Maggie stormed out of the store, Alex turned to his wife. "I don't envy that lad."

"Don't pity the boy, Alex," Lucy replied. "It's her who's hurting."

Iain was standing at the corner, his hands in his pockets and back to the shop. Maggie wished he didn't look so handsome even from behind.

"Hey, Grant!" she yelled. "Here's your check. Come and get it."

Iain turned and shook his head. Slowly he walked back to where Maggie stood holding his check over her head. A futile gesture. He was a good half-foot taller than her.

"Don't Maggie," he said. "Just don't."

"Edinburgh?" she demanded. "What's in Edinburgh?"

He shrugged. "A fresh start, I suppose."

"Why do you need a fresh start?" she demanded. "You've got a life here. A job. Friends. But you're going to run away at the first sign of trouble?"

"It's a bit more complicated than that," Iain replied.

"No, it's not. You're scared, so you're running away."

Iain shook his head and ran a hand through that black hair of his. "You lied to me, Maggie."

Maggie pulled herself up. "I didn't lie," she insisted.

Iain sighed. "That's all you did. Everything was a lie. All of the trips, all of the talks, all of the..." He let the thought trail off. "You never told me what was really going on. You still haven't. You've never told me truth."

Maggie wasn't sure how to reply. Her hand holding the check slowly lowered. "Well... I mean... Can you blame me?"

Iain thought for a moment, then nodded. "Aye. I can blame you."

"You wouldn't have believed me," Maggie accused.

Iain shook his head. "You're wrong. I believed all the lies. I certainly would have believed the truth."

Maggie lowered her voice. "So you believe it?"

"Of course." Iain managed a mirthless chuckle. "I can believe my own eyes, even if I can't believe you."

Maggie thought for a moment. "You're not going to tell anyone, are you?"

Iain cocked his head and frowned. "That's what you care about? Whether I tell someone about your little secret?"

Maggie felt her heart clench. "No. Well, yes. I mean, not *just* that."

Iain raised his palm to interrupt her. "Well, don't worry yourself, Miss Devereaux. Your secret is safe with me."

A horn honked and Maggie noticed for the first time the mini convertible idling a few cars down from the front of the shop. The driver was a young woman with wispy blond hair and a floral scarf. She pulled off her oversized sunglasses, revealing large, cat-like eyes. "Iain? Are you coming finally?"

The vice around Maggie's heart tightened. "Who's that?" she demanded. She recalled her own question: *'What's in Edinburgh?'*

"A friend," Iain said in a way that left no doubt the woman was more than a friend. "I have to go."

Maggie stood numbly as Iain extracted the check from her grip. She turned and pointed at the door knocker behind her. "What about this?" she asked. "What about 'Be Traist'?"

Iain frowned and shook his head. "That's your clan's motto, Maggie. Not mine. Mine is 'Stand Fast.'" He sighed and turned away. "Goodbye, Maggie."

Maggie could only watch as Iain folded his large body into the other woman's sports car. The woman glanced back at Maggie, then planted a kiss on Iain's check before darting out into the roadway and driving away.

"*Mo cridhe*," Maggie whispered to herself. "My heart. There goes my heart."

7. Body of Evidence

The two police officers burst out of the stairwell, one smiling the other gasping for air.

"Bloody Hell," wheezed the gasper, Officer Thomas Haskins, a young, heavy-set man with thick brown hair that stuck up in the back. "That's a lot of stairs, that is. Her flat would have to be on the top floor, wouldn't it?" He wiped the sweat from his brow. "Well, I'm taking the lift down."

His partner, Officer Jack MacKinney, chuckled. He was the shorter of the two men, thinner with thick biceps. "Come on, then, Tommy, it's good for you. Gotta stay in shape. Taking the lift down won't save you any energy, you know, so it's good you took the stairs coming up."

Haskins shook his thick head. "Aye, well, I guess it was only two flights." He stopped to take in a deep breath. "But I'm telling you, Jack, I've either got to get in better shape or find a new partner."

"Keep me as your partner, Tommy, and you'll get in better shape." MacKinney pulled up in front of the last door on the left. "Here we are. Flat number twelve."

"And why are we here again?" Haskins panted, holding his side.

"Welfare check," MacKinney replied. "The caller said there

was a bad smell coming from inside."

Haskins took a deep sniff. "Aye." He nodded. "I smell something too."

MacKinney frowned. "Aye."

They'd both been cops long enough to recognize the smell.

MacKinney knocked on the door anyway. "Hello? Is anyone home? This is the police. Please open the door."

Nothing. Which is exactly what they expected.

Another knock-and-announce. Again, no response.

"I suppose we can go in now," Haskins said. He reached into his pocket and extracted the master key the landlord had given them.

MacKinney nodded and stepped aside for Haskins to open the door. Haskins slipped the key in to the lock and twisted it without ever checking the door first to see if it was even locked. When he tried to open it, it didn't budge, so he turned the key all the way the other direction and felt the deadbolt pop. He finally pushed the door open with a sheepish grin.

But any further thoughts about the difficulty in opening the door were swept away by the overpowering smell that rushed out of the darkened flat.

"Oh." Haskins covered his nose and turned away. "That's rank."

MacKinney grimaced against the stench. He nodded but elected not to reply, lest he breathe in more than absolutely necessary. He jerked his head toward the apartment and the two officers stepped inside.

Although it was the middle of a sunny afternoon, the flat was dim. All the shades were drawn and the lights off. They crept in slowly, glancing around, wondering not so much what they'd find, but where they'd find it.

The answer, after a cursory search of the kitchen and living room, was the master bedroom. It was a two-bedroom flat, comfortably furnished and nicely decorated—save the corpse suspended by its neck on the bedroom closet door.

"Oh," Haskins said again through his hand. "There she is."

His first instinct was to take the body down, but MacKinney grabbed his arm. "Leave her there, Tommy. She's beyond help. The detectives will want to see the room exactly as we found it."

Haskins frowned. "I suppose you're right," he admitted, again through his hand, pressed even tighter in such close proximity to the decaying body. He peered up at the lifeless face of the dead woman. Her eyes were wide open, bulging out, criss-crossed in red with the broken blood vessels that accompany strangulation when the blood can't get out of the head again. Her tongue, also swollen, jutted out slightly, and her skin was already starting to stretch and mummify in the heat of the stuffy flat.

"I wonder what she looked like when she alive," Haskins said.

MacKinney shrugged. "A hell of a lot better than she does now, I'd wager." He turned away and scanned the room. "Ah, there it is."

"What?" Haskins asked, also turning from the distorted corpse hanging off the floor.

"The suicide note," MacKinney answered. He was standing at the small writing desk on the other side of the bedroom. Haskins joined his partner and read over his shoulder.

I'm sorry. I just couldn't bear it anymore. God forgive me.

MacKinney frowned. "Not a lot of detail," he observed.

"Oh, so you're going to criticize a woman's last thoughts

before she kills herself?" Haskins scolded. "That's cold."

MacKinney shrugged. "Well, it's hot in here. And it stinks. Let's go. The detectives can do the clean up."

Haskins agreed and they stepped toward the exit. But as they left the bedroom, Haskins turned around and, looking up again at the dead woman, he crossed himself.

8. Message in a Bottle

The next few weeks brought both clarity and confusion. Her patchy memory slowly solidified until she could remember everything up to Iain walking away under Visegrád Castle, and everything after waking up in the Edinburgh hotel. But just as clearly as she could remember all that, she could absolutely not remember anything at all during those missing Lost Weeks. It was a hole in her memory, its edges as sharp and clearly defined as a picture frame.

Similarly, her emotions came into focus. Her disbelief at Iain fleeing to Edinburgh with some blonde floozy crystallized into angry betrayal. Her vague comfort at returning home coalesced into welcome stability. And her anxiety at having lost her Dark Book solidified into abject panic.

She could worry about Iain later. Or not.

But she had to find the Dark Book.

The only problem was that she had absolutely no idea where to start. But she remembered reading once that the best place to start is at the beginning. So early one morning, after a sensible breakfast of cereal, coffee, and a banana, she pulled her backpack over her shoulders and headed for the university, hoping to find some clue as to the fate of her fortuitously found, and mysteriously lost, grimoire.

She stepped out into a bright, September morning, and locked the door behind her—just before her laptop alerted the arrival of a new email that would prove to be the real clue she was after.

* * *

She took the long way to campus. Not because she didn't want to get there right away, but because she wanted to reconnect with the city. Even though most of her memories had returned, she still felt a vague dissociation. As if the memories were someone else's, or scenes from a movie she'd seen. In any case, walking through the streets and quays of the district surrounding the university helped to push the dissociated unease to the edge of her consciousness. Stepping onto the campus grounds kicked it over that edge. She was home. Or at least, she was where she was happiest. On campus.

The skyline was dominated by the stone crown sitting astride the arches atop the King's College Building. She followed it like a Wise Man after a star. Her destination lay tucked between the King's College building and the equally impressive Elphinstone Hall with its gothic turrets and arched doorways.

But the real prize was between the two buildings, a smallish construct bearing a plaque with the simple yet glorious words:

HISTORIC COLLECTIONS
MANUSCRIPTS AND ARCHIVES

Maggie recalled the first time she stepped into the building, grateful for the treasure she'd found then, and relieved for her current ability to remember.

The main reading room was just as impressive as it had been that first time she'd walked in nearly a year ago, but it was decidedly less populated. September had arrived and the semester was approaching, but the term wouldn't start until the end of the month. The campus held that anticipatory sort of busy which a university takes on when classes are imminent, but preparations are still incomplete. There were a few students, some faculty, and luckily for Maggie just then, most of the staff. She walked to the circulation desk and was greeted by the same heavy-set, gray-haired, and bespectacled woman who'd first given her a key to the university's ancient book collection the previous fall.

"Well, hello again," the woman said as Maggie stepped up. "It's nice to see you again."

Maggie was impressed at the woman's memory. For Maggie, there was only the one—well, maybe two—'women who worked at the historic collections circulation desk.' But Maggie was just one of literally thousands of students at the school.

"Thanks," Maggie replied, a smile blossoming on her face. After everything that had happened since waking up in Edinburgh, it was nice to be remembered. "I'm back."

The woman smiled, squinching her eyes behind her dark-framed glasses. "I can see that. Headed for the ancient book collection again, are you?"

Maggie nodded. "Yes. Is it still in the sub-basement?"

"Oh, aye," the woman laughed. "We couldn't have moved it all in that short of time. Far too many books in far too delicate a condition."

Maggie recalled the fragile state of some of the older books she'd seen on the dim shelves. "Can I go down today? I know the semester hasn't started yet."

The librarian waved the suggestion away. "Of course. You're a doctoral student, aye? You have access whenever you need it, as long as the building is open, that is."

Maggie considered the early hour and supposed she was

unlikely to return upstairs after closing time like on her first visit. "Thanks. I don't expect it will take long."

"Enjoy yourself," the woman replied. "I'll be here if you need anything."

Maggie thanked the woman again then headed for the stone steps that descended beneath the building toward the sub-basement and the treasure vault that had once held her Dark Book. She hoped it might again—although if it did, she'd be faced with the mystery of who had returned it.

The aged stone steps quickly gave way to the ugly modern steps that truly led to the ancient book collection. The study carrels on floor B-3 were vacant and she passed no students sitting between the stacks reading whatever tome they'd pulled from the library's lower floors. It was deathly silent as her shoes clacked to the back of the room and she found herself standing before the wooden door marked with small black, painted letters:

ANCIENT BOOK COLLECTION

She pulled off her backpack. The first time, she'd brought a notepad, pens, her grandmother's book of Old Gaelic literature, and a bottle of water. Each had proved useful in its own way. This time she brought the one thing she'd need: a flashlight.

It was dark in that corner.

She pulled her keys from her pocket and unlocked the door. She turned the switch bolted to the cement wall and waited for the loud electric buzz to activate the aging light fixtures, one crackle-buzz-pop at a time.

Maggie surveyed the room as it lit up, section by section. As far as she could tell, nothing had changed since her last visit. Or her first, for that matter. The four bookshelves still stood against the far wall, the three rows of lights hanging off-center enough to cast the last row into unhelpful darkness. The single table and anachronistic card catalog seemed to be coated with same layer of dust she'd encountered the previous fall. She even craned her neck half-expecting to see a clean spot on the floor from spilt water. But there was no indication the floor had ever been anything but uniformly dusty.

The room appeared undisturbed, but really it simply absorbed its disturbances the way all ancient places do.

She narrowed her eyes and realized that her memory of the room was almost too vivid. It was a welcome change from her the vague, incomplete, or entirely absent memories she had endured for the first days after The Lost Weeks, but it was disconcerting in its own way. She could recall details from a year ago which naturally should have faded. It was almost as if whatever had caused her to lose certain memories had also strengthened the memories that remained. Like a broken bone that, once set and knitted, was stronger than it had been before.

She lingered on the thought of a healed bone for a few seconds as it prompted a new thought to take hold. She glanced at the last, dark row where her present quest ended. Then she looked at the perfectly illuminated first row. It would be a quick detour, she decided, and one she felt suddenly compelled to follow.

She stretched her left hand out against the wall and began a slow descent down the worn steps, without the benefit of a handrail on either side, and a painful drop-off onto the card catalogue threatened to the right. Her hand traced the stone wall, the sticky dust lightly coating her fingertips as her eyes fixed themselves on that first row, and the book she knew was there.

Or not.

Its call number was 'Art.-1.' She recalled that as if it had just been whispered in her ear. And she remembered the title as well: *'Deailbh ann an Alba anns a' Seachdamh Linn Deug,'* Gaelic for

'Painting in Seventeenth Century Scotland.' And she recalled the painting of the noblewoman within, labeled, in Gaelic, 'A Healer. 1621.'

She also remembered where it was situated on the shelf, immediately after 'Arch.-1.' and so she was absolutely certain that she hadn't overlooked it when she reached the place it should have been and it was absolutely, definitely not there.

"Checked out," she muttered. By some art history major, no doubt. She would have cursed the uselessness of such a course of studies if she herself had not been a graduate student in Celtic languages. Not exactly the next big hiring trend, she knew.

Her mouth tightened into a puckered frown and she shrugged, forcing herself to be content with waiting to see the portrait of her ancestor, Brìghde Innes. The Healer.

She could feel a small spark of rage within her at not getting what she wanted, and wondered at it, recalling similar emotions after using the magic. But she knew she hadn't used the magic since she'd awoken in Edinburgh. How could she? The Dark Book was missing.

Then again, she had mastered some of the spells enough to cite them without referring to the source material. For a moment she considered trying to levitate a book off the shelf, just to see if she could, but then she recalled her last nightmare and thought better of it.

Instead, she refocused her attention on her true goal, and extracted her flashlight from her backpack. She wasn't going to stumble again on the uneven floor. And, she decided as she looked down at the tool, she still wasn't going to call it a 'torch.' It was a flashlight. Cultural assimilation had its limits. Words had import. She wouldn't be needing a torch until the next time she stormed a castle.

With a grin, she wondered whether that might not happen sooner than she expected. It had been a hell of year, almost literally.

She exited the first row and proceeded directly to the last row, trading the bright lights directly overhead the art and architecture books, for the shadow cast over the religion books by the unfortunate placement of lights directly above, and inches away from the top of, the third bookshelf.

She shined her flashlight into the recess and smiled. She knew the Dark Book almost certainly wasn't there. But she hoped it was anyway. And either way, it was nice to be back in a place that no one else knew about. Not even Iain or Sinclair. They might have had an inkling about the magic. Might have seen it in action, still doubtful of their own eyes. But no one else had been in this corner; no one knew where she had found the Book; no one else knew the importance of this lost place beneath a forgettable building.

She walked in slowly, illuminating the floor. There was the uneven stone she had tripped over. There was the row of books on the bottom corner. There was where the light from above completely disappeared as the call numbers reached 'Rel. Gael.-7.'

She knelt down onto the hard, dirty floor. The light shone on the gap between 'Rel.Gael.-6' and 'Rel. Gael-8.' Just as she had suspected. It wasn't there.

She'd had to look, but it wasn't there.

And just as her mind started down the road of next possibilities, it was pulled back by the slightest reflection of light from within the depths of the shelf.

Bending down so her cheek was almost on the cool stone of the floor, she flashed the light in again and confirmed a book tucked behind the others. A familiar situation.

Disturbingly so.

She reached in and pulled out the book.

It wasn't her Dark Book. She had known that as soon as she had spied the white binding. Her hand confirmed it was also considerably thinner and lighter than her Dark Book. Nevertheless she pulled it out and appraised the cover, her surprise almost greater than it would have been had she actually been holding her Dark Book.

It was the missing art history book. 'Painting in Seventeenth Century Scotland.' The title was actually in Gaelic. So was the note tucked in at Brìghde's portrait.

"Don't believe it's gone," Maggie translated aloud. "She didn't."

What's gone? she wondered. *And who didn't believe it?*

Maggie thought she might know the answers. Then she set her mind to the bigger question: who could have known to leave such a note for her. She thought she knew that answer too.

"Sarah."

* * *

"Sarah MacKenzie."

The visiting inspector from Edinburgh announced the name as if Warwick should have recognized it somehow. It was familiar enough to the Aberdeen sergeant, but Sarah was hardly an uncommon name, and MacKenzie was one of the larger clans in Scotland. The name was like a Highland 'Joan Smith.'

Warwick had been relieved when Cameron had pulled her from her perusal of the grave-robbing file. She wasn't happy that someone was defiling graves in her city, but she would have preferred using her skills to solve, even prevent, more recent deaths. When Cameron had told her an inspector from Edinburgh had arrived, wanting to discuss a recent murder that appeared to have ties to Aberdeen, Warwick spied an opportunity to shove the grave-robbing case off onto Sergeant Willis or someone else who could handle a case where the cause of death wasn't at issue.

"Who's Sarah MacKenzie?" Warwick asked, the name still tickling the back of her brain.

"She's a professor at the University of Aberdeen," Inspector Lindsey Benson answered. "And her cellular number was the last one our victim telephoned before he was murdered."

9. I Demand an Explanation

Warwick's expression didn't change. She knew how to keep a poker face. But her stomach twinged. The name had sounded familiar, but when Warwick mentally linked murder with the university, it was another woman's name that came to mind. Especially this type of murder.

"Can you describe again," she asked her colleague from Edinburgh, "how the body was found? I don't think I was listening as closely as I should have done."

Cameron raised an eyebrow at her. They'd been working together long enough for him to note the rarity of the admission—or the need for it.

Benson nodded. It was a strange enough murder. Warwick knew that Benson had likely had to explain it more than once to more than one person.

"The body was found in a bathtub, prone, face up. He'd suffered blunt force trauma to the back of his head and there was blood everywhere."

"And this was at a hotel?" Warwick confirmed.

"Right," Benson answered. "The Hotel Regency. The room was rented to a 'Devan Sinclair.'"

Warwick was pretty sure her poker face cracked slightly at that name. She covered it with a quick cough.

"We're still trying to track him down," Benson offered. "His last known address was Aberdeen, so perhaps you can help with that as well."

"I'm sure we can," Cameron assured.

Warwick pushed back to the crime scene. "How do you know the dead man wasn't this Devan Sinclair?"

"His driver's license, for starters," Benson explained. "Derek Peabody of Vancouver, Canada. Plus, one of the maids said she had a brief conversation with him in the lobby. He said he was Canadian, and had the accent to match. Said he'd come to Scotland to work, but she couldn't remember as what. Something dry and boring, she said."

"How'd she recognize him?" Warwick asked. "You didn't bring her to the room, did you?"

"Oh, good Lord, no," Benson insisted. "That's no place for civilians. Apart from contaminating the scene, I'm not going to burn that into some cleaning girl's memory forever. No, we showed her a photo the coroner took. After they'd cleaned off the blood, and removed that blasted stone."

Warwick heart dropped. "Stone? What stone?"

Benson tapped her chin. "That was the strangest part. The killer placed a small, flat stone on the victim's face—right across the bridge of his nose."

Warwick closed her eyes. It was happening again.

"Actually, no." Benson corrected herself. "That wasn't the strangest part. The strangest part was his spine."

"His spine?" Cameron asked. "What about his spine?"

Benson raised an eyebrow. "It was gone."

* * *

Time to show some backbone, Maggie told herself as she locked the door to the Ancient Book Collection behind her and marched toward the surface. It was one thing for Sarah to have lied to her to gain her sympathy for some twisted cause. It was quite another to poke her in the eye with the fact that she knew Maggie's secret.

Professor Sarah MacKenzie had some explaining to do.

But Maggie was so wrapped up in her righteous indignation that she failed to notice the pair of unpleasantly large feet jutting out from between two of the narrow bookshelves on level B-3. She tripped over them and landed in an even more indignant heap. And with a loud, "Ouch!"

"Watch where you're going there, lad," said a voice from within the bookshelves. The feet recoiled between the shelves and a moment later their owner stepped out to confront her. "You nearly scuffed up my new boots."

Maggie had managed to roll onto her backside, and found herself looking up at the large-footed man. The rest of him was equally unpleasant. He was a bit too tall, and definitely too thin. The skin on his arms seemed to be stretched directly over the bone, with no fat or muscle between. Thick black hair stuck to his head, combed forward from the crown, most likely with his fingers. He wore glasses that were too large and covered in smudges, as were his clothes. She was pretty sure she grimaced when she saw him. But he smiled.

"Oh," he said, exposing a nubby row of surprisingly small teeth, "you're not a lad."

She added a sneer to the grimace. "No," she replied, pulling herself to her feet. "I'm not. How smart of you to notice. You must be a student here."

His nubby smile fairly exploded. "You're an American!"

It sounded like an accusation. She almost went with the 'Canadian' line again, but thought better of it. Instead she stayed with snarky. "Brilliant, professor. How do you do it?"

"An American lass trips over my feet," the too-tall man said to no one in particular. "And a pretty one at that. How lucky can a lad get?"

You're not getting lucky with me, Maggie thought. "I'm going to go now," she announced.

He ignored her threat. "I'm Stuart." He stuck out his hand. "Stuart Menzies. I'm a student here at the college."

Maggie regarded the hand. It was strangely small compared to the lanky frame and large feet. After a moment's revulsion, she relented and shook it. It was clammy.

"Maggie Devereaux," she managed to say. "I'm a student here too."

"Are you then?" Stuart didn't let go of her hand. She had to pull it out, which wasn't hard given the dampness of his palm. He held up a book. The cover read 'The Unabridged History of Science.' "You don't study science by any chance, do you?"

"Afraid not," Maggie was relieved to say. She'd feared he was another languages student. God forbid she ever run into him again. She turned to leave. "Bye."

Stuart lowered his book. "Oh. Right, then. Okay, well, bye, Maggie Devereaux, pretty American student. I'll see you around then, shall I?"

"Not if I see you first," she muttered under her breath as she hurried to the stairway that led back up to the main hall.

She barely managed a perfunctory nod to the woman behind the circulation desk on her way out of the building. Easily pushing thoughts of Stuart Menzies out of her head, she strode purposefully toward the Taylor Building, home of the college's modern language programs. More importantly, it was home to the offices of the professors in the college's modern language programs. Most importantly, it was home to Sarah MacKenzie's office.

She yanked open the outer doors and stormed up the steps, not even thinking to look at the reader board to see whether they'd replaced all the missing 'i's yet. She knew where MacKenzie's office was. She knew what MacKenzie was doing. She knew exactly what she was going to say to her.

But when she got the office, she had absolutely no idea who the dashing young man inside was.

"Hello," he said when he noticed her, standing slack-jawed in the doorway. "Can I help you?"

He was tall, but not too tall, with sandy brown hair, dark sideburns, and an obviously athletic body hidden under a casually professional button-up shirt and khakis. His accent was like hers.

"You're, you're not Sarah MacKenzie," Maggie observed.

The dashing young man laughed, but kindly. "No, I'm definitely not." He extended his hand. "I'm Philip Harmon. I'm a visiting professor from the University of British Columbia in Vancouver, Canada."

Maggie took his hand. It was soft but strong. The hand of an academic, but a confident one.

"Maggie," she managed to reply. "Maggie Devereux."

He'd noticed her accent of course. "Are you Canadian too?"

Maggie smiled as she appraised Philip Harmon's high cheek bones and deep brown eyes. "Sure."

* * *

"Totally spineless?" Warwick asked incredulously.

"No, not totally," Benson clarified. "It looked that way at the scene, but once we got the body to the morgue, the coroner was able to take a compete inventory. There were seven vertebrae missing, basically everything below his rib-cage."

"It's symbolic," Warwick opined.

"You think so?" Benson questioned.

"Clearly. It's the base of his spine. The backbone. The strongest part of something. When you build something, you talk about constructing its backbone first, then adding on."

"So what are they building?" Benson asked.

"I don't know," Warwick admitted. "But there's another question."

"What's that?"

"Why this man? Was he important, particular? Or was he just a random victim? If so, why pick a healthy man in the prime of his life? He'd be the last person to target if you wanted to kill just anyone. Too much ability to fight back."

Benson nodded. "You're right. He was chosen specifically."

"So," Warwick said, "we need to find out what's so special about a young Canadian man who'd come to Scotland to work in a dry and boring field."

* * *

Philip laughed again. "'Sure'?" he questioned.

Maggie shook off her bedazzlement. "Uh, right. I mean, no. Not Canadian. American. But I'm from Seattle, so that's pretty close to Canada."

"Very close," Philip agreed. Maggie noticed they were still holding hands. "Practically neighbors."

Maggie smiled as their hands finally parted.

"So, are you a visiting professor too?" he asked.

Maggie felt a blush and she looked down. "No, I'm just a student."

Philip shook his head. "There's no such thing as just a student. We're all students, all our lives."

Maggie looked up and smiled.

Philip raised an appraising eyebrow. "Besides, I'd wager you'll be a professor soon enough."

Maggie's blush deepened. She shrugged. "I dunno. Maybe."

"So did you just arrive in Aberdeen too?"

"Uh, no," she felt proud to answer. "I've been here a year already."

And what a year! she thought.

"Well, then you are the master and I am the pupil," Philip said. He folded his laptop closed and pushed it to the back of his desk, then gestured toward the hallway and what lay beyond. "I haven't had a chance to tour the campus yet. Would you be willing to educate a neighbor a bit about the local scenery?"

Maggie smiled and appraised the scenery herself.

"Absolutely."

* * *

"Absolutely no leads on the killer though," Benson frowned. "Except for this one clue."

She reached into her pocket and extracted a plastic bag. It was sealed at the top with red evidence tape, but the baggie was clear and the contents were quite visible.

Inside was a single piece of jewelry: a silver pendant of the crest of the Clan Innes, with its boar's head and motto, 'Be Traist.'

"We find the owner of this," Benson posited, "and I wager we've found our killer."

10. Hanging Propositions

After a brief tour of the campus buildings closest to Taylor, Maggie took Philip to her favorite coffee shop. Well, one of them anyway. The one closest to campus, for when she needed a quick boost before a night of library-dwelling.

"My treat," she insisted as they stepped inside. The trust fund from her grandmother was in good shape. She hadn't gotten around to investing any of it, which had turned out to be a good thing in light of recent financial events. Her principal was intact.

Philip started to protest, but elected to turn conflict into opportunity. "Fine. But next time, I buy."

Maggie smiled. 'Next time.' She liked the sound of that. "Deal."

Despite a year in Scotland, she was still a Seattle girl, and often eschewed tea for a good, strong cup of coffee. Especially at mid-morning when she needed a bit of energy. She was pleased to see her North American colleague followed suit.

"Tea is fine," he said as he ordered a large black coffee, "but living in Vancouver, you need coffee to get through the winter."

"Ah, yes. The Northwest rainy season," Maggie joked as they found a table in the corner. "September through June."

Philip laughed. "Exactly. Although I suppose the weather is

similar here in Scotland?"

Maggie shrugged. "A bit. It rains plenty, but the winter seems dryer and colder than Seattle. It usually snows, I think."

Philip nodded and smiled at her over his ceramic cup. "Well, that's one more thing to look forward to this year."

Maggie enjoyed his smile, and the suggestion behind his comment. But there was a problem, she knew. "So, you're a professor."

She couldn't date a professor.

"Er, yes," Philip stammered. He knew the rules too, of course. "Just visiting this year." As if that mattered. It didn't. Not if she took any classes from him, anyway.

"What will you be teaching?" Maggie asked as she sipped from her still scalding beverage.

Philip raised his eyebrows and shrugged. "I'm not sure actually," he admitted. "My specialty is dialect variations in Old Gaelic, but—"

Maggie sat forward. "Excuse me. What did you just say?"

Philip offered a surprised smile. "Um, my specialty is dialect variations in Old Gaelic. Especially non-traditional orthographic mutations. Why?"

Why? Maggie repeated in her head, staring at the handsome young academic with the shared interest. But who was, nevertheless, a professor and therefore off-limits. *Why indeed?*

"Oh, it's just, that's kind of my area of interest too."

"Really?" Philip leaned forward on to the table as well. Their faces were only a foot or two apart. "You know, I saw a brochure in my new office about a conference next month dealing exclusively with Old Gaelic language and literature. The keynote speaker is Professor Robert Hamilton of the University of Edinburgh. Are you familiar with him? I really admire his work."

Wow. Maggie was about to reply, 'Oh, yes,' and enthuse about Hamilton's theory of a lost dialect of Old Gaelic used for religious ceremonies. She might even have let her guard down a bit too much and suggested she not only agreed with him, but had stumbled upon actual source material. There was something about those brown eyes across the table from her. Something about being in the company of a kindred soul. An academic, with shared interests, from her part of the world. Her defenses were melting. She could practically feel it. Luckily, before she could say too much—or say anything at all, for that matter—her friend Ellen Walker burst onto the scene.

"Maggie!" she shouted from the entrance door, still ajar against her back heel. "There you are!"

She rushed over to Maggie and Philip's table, although she seemed oblivious to Maggie's companion. "Where have you been? I've been worried sick. I talked to Iain and—"

"Hello, Ellen," Maggie quickly interrupted. She gestured across the table. "This is Philip Harmon. He's teaching at the college this year."

Ellen finally turned to the other person at the table. "Oh. Um. Right." She smiled, but only slightly, so her strong teeth were mostly hidden behind her still processing expression. "Hello."

"Hello," Philip replied cordially. "It's nice to meet you." Then he turned to Maggie. "Have you been missing lately?"

Maggie pasted a smile on her face. "Oh, no. Of course not. I'm sure I've been exactly where I was supposed to be. Wherever that might have been."

Philip grinned at the cryptic comment. Ellen's smile broadened. She offered a wink to the professor. "Our Maggie's a wee bit mysterious."

"Is that right?" Philip asked, narrowing his gaze to his coffee companion.

Maggie's own smile tightened. "Ellen..."

Philip took a casual sip of his coffee. Keeping his eyes downcast, he asked, "Who's Iain?"

Ellen took in a breath to start her own explanation, but Maggie spoke first. "No one," she assured. "He's no one."

Ellen looked askance at Maggie. So Maggie changed the subject. "Professor Harmon's specialty is lost dialects of Old Gaelic."

Ellen's expression was duly impressed. She knew that was Maggie's dissertation topic. "Is that right? So will you be teaching courses on that this year? I know a lass who'd love to study under you, so to speak. Sit right in the front row, she would."

Maggie closed her eyes and looked away. She decided to count to ten before she said anything else. In Gaelic, of course.

A h-aon, a dhà, a trì ...

Philip was polite enough to ignore the suggestiveness of Ellen's comments. "Yes, well, I'm not entirely sure yet what I'll be teaching. There's been a change of plan apparently."

Maggie opened her eyes. She hadn't reached *a deich*, but there was something in how Philip had said that. "Change of plan?" she asked.

Philip nodded. "Yes. It's kind of a long story, but apparently I'm going to be taking on some courses previously taught by a Professor MacKenzie."

Maggie's raised eyebrows were more than trumped by Ellen's loud gasp. Maggie remembered that she'd found Philip in Sarah's office. She'd been so taken by the sight of him, she'd forgotten all about MacKenzie.

"*Sarah* MacKenzie?" Maggie confirmed.

"Yes, I believe that was it," Philip answered. "They told me they needed me to take over most of her classes, but they didn't say why."

"They didn't even tell you?" Ellen practically shouted.

"No," Philip replied. "Tell me what?"

"What's going on, Ellen?" Maggie asked. Ellen was clearly agitated.

"They should have told you," Ellen said to Philip.

"Told him what, Ellen?" Maggie pressed.

Ellen looked at Maggie, her eyes wide. Then they relaxed just a bit and she nodded. "Oh, that's right. You've been gone. You wouldn't know."

"Wouldn't know what?" Philip asked.

"Professor MacKenzie," Ellen answered. She shook her head, then looked down and crossed herself. "Professor MacKenzie is dead."

* * *

"Dead?" Benson's tone suggested more irritation at the complication than remorse at the event. "Are you certain?"

"Quite certain." Warwick nodded. "She was quite dead. Hanged herself. I knew that name was familiar when you mentioned it. A university professor committing suicide is big news, around here anyway. One of the college administrators let it slip he was glad it happened during the summer holiday."

"Very nice," Cameron observed.

"Academics can be fairly ruthless, I've found," Warwick said. "A lot of back-stabbing and pressure. She probably just cracked."

Benson put a hand to her chin and narrowed her gaze at Warwick. "Is that what you think happened?"

Warwick returned the look, a professional smile creeping into the corner of her mouth. "No. I didn't think much of that theory then. Now, I think even less of it."

"When did she die?" Benson inquired.

Warwick pursed her lips in thought, comparing her information with Benson's. "I believe we found our body right after your murder. But she'd already been dead a few days."

"So, the question is," Benson posited, "why did a dead man call someone who was already dead herself?"

"Answer that," Cameron said, "and you'll solve both cases."

Warwick didn't know enough yet to think, *All three cases.*

11. Claim Check

Warwick held open the front door of the late Sarah MacKenzie's apartment complex. Benson stepped out onto the sidewalk and toward their waiting patrol car.

"I thought that visit would be more useful," Benson complained.

"It's been pretty well cleaned up now," Warwick admitted. "The landlord's eager to rent it out again, and we didn't know then it'd be linked to a murder in another city."

"Pity that," Benson remarked as she grabbed the car's door handle. "Too late to process the scene properly."

Warwick could only nod as she too slipped into the car. She started the engine. "There's probably still something in there, but we'd have to know what we were looking for to find it." She regretted the statement as a possible admission of sub-standard work. "I mean, we did process it appropriately. It came in as just another suicide."

Benson shrugged and gazed out the windshield. "So where are we going now?"

"To test that theory," Warwick replied.

"What theory?"

"That it was just another suicide," Warwick answered.

"Let's pay a visit to the coroner."

* * *

The coroner's office was located in the ground floor of the city morgue. Benson thought that might be a good thing, judging by the advanced years and generally frail appearance of the Aberdeen Coroner, Dr. Andrew Wood. A short trip to the basement freezers when he succumbed himself, an event which appeared, at least at first blush, to be imminent. However, after a few minutes with the slightly built physician, his thin white sweater matching his wispy white curls, it became clear he wasn't going anywhere any time soon.

"Elizabeth!" he called out from behind his desk as the two officers walked into his office. He pulled himself to his feet and stepped around to greet his guests. "What an unexpected delight. Who's your friend?"

"Lindsey Benson," the detective introduced herself. "Edinburgh Police Department."

"Oh!" Wood exclaimed. "Edinburgh, eh? Must be important to warrant an emissary from our glorious capital city."

Benson smiled at Wood's effusiveness. "I'm afraid not. Just another murder. But it might be connected to Aberdeen."

Wood shook his head and frowned. "There's no such thing as just another murder."

Benson had to agree. "Of course. That's not what I meant, exactly."

Warwick decided to jump in before a turn of phrase turned into an argument. "Well, to the extent there can be just another murder, this one wasn't it. Body parts missing and a stone across his eyes."

The geniality drained from Wood's expression. "Oh," he repeated, but it meant something entirely different. "Again?"

Warwick shrugged. "Maybe. That's why we're here."

"We haven't had any more murders like that, Elizabeth. You'd know that."

Benson looked between her companions, her expression betraying her lack of understanding. They didn't bother to explain to her.

"I do know that, Andy," Warwick replied. "And I'm hoping it stays that way. But this might have a connection to us anyway."

Wood stood up straighter and tugged the wrinkles out of his sweater. "What can I do to help?"

"Do you recall an autopsy on a Sarah MacKenzie?" Warwick asked. "She hanged herself. Happened last month."

Wood shook his head. "I do a lot of autopsies, Elizabeth. And the staff does even more. I don't recall it off the top of my head."

But the old doctor shuffled to the file cabinet in the coroner of his office and pulled open the middle drawer. "Let me see if it's still here. Our new secretary keeps nagging me about going paperless and scanning and other witchcraft, but I like a good old-fashioned report in my hand." He thumbed through the files in the drawer. "Ah, here we are. MacKenzie, Sarah Marie."

He opened the file and began reading, but didn't bother the few steps back to the officers. After a moment he looked up with a sardonic grin. "Just another suicide."

That broke the tension a bit. "No such thing, doctor?" Benson ventured.

Wood smiled. "Correct. But, nothing that stood out either." His younger visitors stepped over to where he stood. "Hanged herself over a door. Terrible way to go really."

"Oh yeah?" Benson encouraged.

"Yes," Wood answered. "There was a reason they built those

gallows. When you dropped through the trap door, your neck would break. That's what killed you. But slowly strangling to death is a difficult end. People often fail at it because the agony is too much and they abort the attempt. Piece of advice." He looked up at Benson, then Warwick. "If you're going to kill yourself, just tie a plastic bag over your head. You'll fall asleep and never wake up. Simple."

"Great." Benson cringed. "Thanks."

"So she must have been very intent on killing herself," Warwick ignored the coroner's so-called advice. "She didn't abort the attempt, so to speak."

Wood looked down again at the file to confirm. "No, there was no apparent effort to stop. Simple strangulation by the ligature. Sometimes we see scratches at the throat where the person made some last ditch effort to claw at the rope, but there was nothing like that here."

"Did you check her fingernails for DNA?" Benson asked.

"DNA?" Wood scoffed. "No, ma'am. As I said, it was just another suicide. Why run DNA on her fingernails if it's just going to come back as her own? We already had her DNA."

Warwick cocked her head. "You typed her DNA? Why would you do that? To identify her?"

Wood closed the file and shook his head. "No, no. That's not what I meant. I meant, we had no need to do any sort of testing because we already had her body. We could get all the DNA we'd ever want, but what's the point in a suicide?"

Good question, Warwick thought. Then she clenched her jaw. She had one more question. She already knew the answer, and hated it. "Where's the body, Andy?"

Wood shrugged. "Cremated," he answered, confirming Warwick's fear. "Of course."

Warwick nodded. "Of course."

* * *

It was time for lunch. Warwick pointed the car toward one of the business districts near the college and a few minutes later they had parked and were walking to a cheap sandwich place Warwick knew. As they did so, they walked past a local tourist shop with tartans and clan memorabilia in the window. Benson grabbed Warwick's arms and brought them to an abrupt halt.

"Look at that." Benson pointed at a display table covered in pins and other jewelry.

Warwick nodded at the display but was uncertain what to say. Benson reached into her shoulder bag and pulled out the evidence baggie with the Innes Clan crest pendant. "Those are just like this one."

Warwick appraised the pendant in Benson's hand and the baubles in the window. "Not exactly," she opined. "The ones in the shop are a bit gaudier."

Benson twisted her face up in appraisal, then nodded. "I can't disagree. They obviously know what appeals to the tourists." She grabbed Warwick's arm again and tugged her toward the door. "Let's see what else they know."

And with that, Benson pushed open the door to MacTarys' Woolens Shop.

Lucy MacTary was taking advantage of the pre-lunch lull to straighten the bolts of fabric in the bins that lined the far wall of the shop. When the bells on the door jingled, she turned to greet the two women who had just entered her store.

"Good day, ladies. Can I help you find anything?"

Warwick immediately recognized Lucy MacTary. It hadn't been that long since the string of campus murders. She could still recall the interrogation of Lucy and her husband at their home. She turned away and pretended to peruse whatever might help hide her face while Benson inquired about the pendant. Sometimes it was good when they knew you were a cop; sometimes it wasn't. The trick was knowing which was which.

"I was interested," Benson pointed toward the display in the window, "in the clan crest jewelry."

"Oh, aye." Lucy stepped over to the display table. Warwick slid along the wall toward some seemingly enthralling tweeds. "What are you looking for? A scarf pin, perhaps?"

"A pendant, actually," Benson replied.

"Oh, aye," Lucy repeated in her saleswoman voice. "Those are very popular. We just got in a shipment of ones with small colored jewels embedded at the bottom. Absolutely gorgeous, they are."

Benson shook her head slightly. "No, I'm looking for something a bit simpler. Just silver. And smaller."

Lucy nodded and raised a hand to her chin. She had no such pendants on display, but it was obvious she wasn't going to let that deter her sales pitch. Warwick peered over, but then the curtain to the backroom parted and in walked Lucy's husband, Alex. Warwick turned sharply away and practically buried her face in the tweeds.

"I'm sure I have something you'd like," Lucy pressed on. "Is it a gift for someone with particular tastes?"

"No," Benson answered. "It's more of a replacement for a particular piece."

"I see, I see," Lucy said. "And for which clan is it?"

"Well, you know, I'm not sure." Benson reached into her pocket and extracted the evidence bag again. "Do you recognize this?"

Warwick couldn't resist a peek. Lucy was reaching for the baggie. Alex was reaching for her.

"Maggie's pendant!" Lucy exclaimed. "You found it."

"Maggie who?" Benson demanded.

"Maggie no one," Alex replied first.

"Maggie Devereaux," Warwick said as she finally turned around.

"You!" Lucy pointed at Warwick. "You're that police inspector."

"Sergeant, actually," Warwick corrected. "Sergeant Elizabeth Warwick."

Benson looked askance at Warwick. "Do you know them?"

Warwick nodded. "Yes. We had occasion to meet last fall. About an unpleasant business."

Lucy and Alex had to nod in agreement.

"So Maggie lost her pendant?" Warwick asked.

"Er, no," Lucy realized to say. Then considered just who she was talking to, and the ramifications of lying to them. "That is, uh..."

Alex sidestepped the question. "I'm not sure that's our Maggie's pendant," he opined, squinting at the baggie. "Hers was a cheap knock-off from the States. Probably made in China."

"Ours are made in China too," Lucy admitted absently.

"Hush, love," Alex said. Then he looked to Warwick. "I don't think we can help you."

Warwick nodded. She knew he was right, or at least that they wouldn't be helping them any more than they just had. "Thank you for your time. C'mon, Lindsey. Let's go."

Benson looked like she wanted to protest and continue the questioning, but she deferred to her local host. "All right." She put the pendant away and nodded to the MacTarys. "Good day, then, Thank you."

Lucy and Alex returned the nod and watched the police

officers step out onto the sidewalk.

"Who's Maggie Devereaux?" Benson asked once they were outside.

"It's a long story," Warwick replied. "I'll tell you over lunch."

But she wouldn't be telling her everything.

12. Research Assistance

Maggie broke the plane of her flat almost as dazed as when she'd dropped from the hotel room window in Edinburgh. Sarah MacKenzie dead? Why? How? Did *she* take the Dark Book? Is that why she killed herself? If so, who had the Book now?

And that didn't even count the extra confusion occasioned by the dashing young academic from Canada.

She'd spent the afternoon wandering around campus and the surrounding environs, considering what she'd learned and trying to tease out what it could possibly mean.

Finally home again, she had several questions she wanted to look into. Luckily, research was her strong suit. So, after removing her shoes and using the facilities, she clicked her laptop on and went to the kitchen to make some tea. Research could take a while. She knew the importance of fortifying it with caffeine and comfort.

She poured the boiling water into a small brown teapot and added a silver ball full of loose Earl Gray tea. Then she returned to her computer while the tea steeped. She'd settled on three main areas to investigate:

First, Sarah MacKenzie's suicide. When did it happen? Where? How had she killed herself? Was it really suicide? (Of course it was, she thought, but it seemed the detective-y thing to ask.) Had she gotten ahold of the Dark Book and tried the magic only to have been driven to suicide by the ensuing nightmares? Did she really leave the note in the Ancient Book Collection? Was it some sort of suicide note?

Second, the murder in Edinburgh. She figured enough time had passed for most of the details to have leaked into the press. Who was the victim? Had they identified the killer yet? Had they arrested him? The why of it all, how it related to the murders last fall, and the location of her Book—those were almost certainly not in the papers. But she might be able to glean something from the details that were published.

And third, Philip Harmon. She wasn't stupid. She was going to google his ass.

She sat down at her desk and grabbed the mouse she kept plugged into the laptop when it was on her desk. She was about to click on the internet browser when she noticed she had new email. Despite having spent a good portion of the day with and thinking about Philip Harmon, she couldn't help but wonder whether the email might be from Iain.

She clicked on her email. The answer was definitely no.

The sender's email address chilled her blood almost as much as the subject line:

sarah123@scotmail.com
Do exactly as I say

Maggie stared at the screen for several moments. She knew she needed to open the message, but she was in no particular hurry to do so. She also noticed there were no emails from Iain. But her disappointment at that—and her irritation at her disappointment— was subsumed into her curiosity and apprehension at receiving a potentially threatening email from a dead woman.

She stood up. She was going to need that tea. And maybe something stronger.

A few minutes later, after introducing the good Earl to a certain Mr. Walker, Maggie sat down and again regarded her email account.

Do exactly as I say

Maggie frowned. *Could that be more ominous?* She shrugged and took a sip of her fortified tea. *Well, yes, probably*, she admitted to herself.

She took another sip then clicked on the message to open it. The message was short and sweet, unadorned by any salutation:

I know everything. Do exactly as I say.

1. Stop looking for the Book

2. Don't use the magic

3. Find Sinclair

Maggie took a long drink, rolling the flavor in her mouth before she swallowed.

"Everything, huh?" she asked aloud.

Ordinarily she might not have been impressed. It was just an email. On the other hand, she'd never received an email from a dead person before. And more important than that was the sign off. Not a name. A phrase.

Be traist.

"Well, I'll be damned," she said.

In more ways than one, she knew.

* * *

Maggie lingered over the email as long as anyone could over just nineteen words. In the end, she was genuinely unsure whether she'd follow any of the advice. But she knew one thing: she still had research to do, its importance only increased by the email from The Great Beyond.

She finally opened her browser and set to work. If reports of Sarah's death hadn't been Maggie's priority research topic before, the email cemented its primacy. She quickly surfed to the sites for Aberdeen's main newspaper and television stations. She started with the TV stations because, as she quickly confirmed, the stories were short and few. Although the suicide of a local professor was newsworthy when it broke, it didn't rate much follow up coverage. There was one story, from the day her body was discovered. A field reporter was standing in front of a random university building—nowhere near Taylor, Maggie noted with some disdain—reporting, mainly, that the police hadn't released many details. The clip lasted thirty seconds and included less information than Ellen had provided at the coffee shop.

Closing out and returning to the newspaper site, Maggie hoped to find at least a little more information. She found three articles. The first was from the same day as the television report and included no additional information. The last was basically an obituary. It was the middle one—a follow-up article published a few days after the first story—that proved to offer at least some further information:

ABERDEEN— Additional details have emerged regarding the apparent suicide of Sarah MacKenzie, professor of Celtic studies at the University of Aberdeen.

Ms. MacKenzie was found deceased in her college district flat three days ago by the police after she failed to appear for work for several days. She had apparently hanged herself over a closet door and had been dead for several days before the discovery of her body.

Neighbors and colleagues were shocked. Ms. MacKenzie had recently returned from holiday abroad and did not seem depressed.

"She was a very nice lady," said one neighbor who asked to remain anonymous. "Always friendly in the hallway. No sign anything was troubling her. Some people can really hide the demons inside them. It's just a shame, it is."

University officials declined to comment.

Memorial services are yet to be scheduled.

Maggie frowned at the screen. A little short on information, but then she hadn't expected much. It confirmed what Ellen had said. Hanging. Yuck. Maggie couldn't imagine slowly strangling to death. Or rather, she could, which made it even worse. Sarah failed at her quest in Hungary, but could that really have made her so despondent to take her own life? Maggie thought, perhaps a bit callously, that Sarah had been made of sterner stuff than that.

The one piece of information that Maggie found the most useful was that it had been several days before the body was discovered. That seemed to preclude that the death had somehow been faked—a possibility, given the email apparently from her former advisor. She expected a person could fake death, but figured it would be substantially more difficult to fake decomposition.

The thought of dead bodies—fresh and rotten—prompted her to move on to her next research topic. Her tea was getting cold anyway. After a quick refill (of both liquids), she sat down again and began topic number two: the murder in Edinburgh.

She was disheartened to see that there was considerably more news coverage of that event than of poor Sarah MacKenzie's suicide. Not simply because the murder of an anonymous man had ranked above the tragedy of a vibrant, if misdirected, woman taking her own life, but also because Maggie had, as she feared, failed to completely avoid detection. The incomprehensible woman in the alley must have spoken with the police after all.

EDINBURGH— Police announced today that they have a person of interest in the recent murder of an unknown man at the Hotel Regency.

The victim was found in a hotel room bathtub, covered in his own blood. The coroner's office reported the cause of death was blunt force trauma to the head. Police have confirmed that the body suffered extensive post-mortem injuries, but refused to elaborate.

The identity of the victim is still unknown. Initial reports suggest he was a foreign tourist, but little else is known at this time.

The person of interest is a young woman seen hurrying from the hotel as the police were arriving. She was described as average height and weight, with brown hair and glasses. She is believed to be Canadian and police therefore believe she may have been the traveling companion of the murder victim.

The only clue to the woman's identity was a pendant left behind at the scene. Police are not releasing details of the pendant at this time in the hope that anyone with special knowledge of such details may be able to shed light on this horrible crime.

Maggie felt a mix of emotions as she finished the article. She was satisfied and relieved that her 'Canadian' ruse had succeeded. But she was disappointed and worried that the police had found her pendant—and a little guilty at having lost it, since it was a gift from her grandmother. She was also amused that the police suspected her to be the victim's traveling partner. Even though she only got a quick glance at his blood-caked face, she was sure she'd never met him before.

Or at least she didn't *remember* meeting him.

Damn The Lost Weeks.

Which led to her last research topic. If there was a foreigner that this fake-Canadian was going to traveling with, it was a certain real-Canadian professor from Vancouver, British Columbia.

And then she suppressed the flood of memories of traveling the Scottish countryside with a certain dark-haired local. Too soon. Too painful.

Instead, she clicked to the search engine and typed in her next research topic.

But much to her chagrin, there were approximately one thousand Philip Harmons, and each one seemed to have his own Facebook, Twitter, and LinkedIn accounts. Even her cybertrip to http://www.ubc.ca proved fruitless. Their faculty page was confusing at best and appeared limited to those professors actually teaching on campus the coming semester. There was no Philip Harmon, but then again, she supposed Philip wasn't teaching at UBC this coming semester.

She could have done more searching, but the whisky was trumping the tea and her eyelids were getting heavy. It had been a long day and she was ready to call it a night. She looked again at the email from Sarah's ghost, then turned off the computer. She was still short on answers but she was glad for one thing: she hadn't used the magic lately. So she could climb into bed reasonably assured she would sleep through the night without any nightmares of empty graves.

13. Graveyard Shift

The shovel made a *shkk* noise as its blade thrust into the earth. The grass roots tore with the turn of the blade. A crescent moon cast the work in a dim, silvery light. The moonlight was coincidental. The moon cycle didn't matter. Not this time.

This time was bigger.

Another shovelful of dirt passed in front of the gravestone. It was slow work, but not as slow as it might have been. And there was time. Time that night, and time until the end of summer. The time halfway between the autumnal equinox and the winter solstice. The time when the veil between the here and the there was at its thinnest.

Time until Samhain.

Time to collect. To prepare. To succeed.

Shkk. Shkk. Shkk.

14. Witch Grave?

Two weeks later, after a fortnight of much thinking, no magic, and nightmare-less dreams, Maggie found herself drinking her morning coffee and lingering over the enigmatic email and its enumerated directives.

1. Stop looking for the Book

2. Don't use the magic

3. Find Sinclair

Working backwards, she couldn't think of any reason to find Sinclair, other than to help her find the Book. And given that Sinclair was unlikely to be found if he didn't want to be, she didn't know how to find him without using the magic.

So the instructions were self-defeating. Not that she was about to be told what to do about her Book and her magic. If she decided to seek out Sinclair, it would be because she wanted to, not because of some cryptic email. She may not have known where the Book was or where Sinclair was or, as she realized with a tinge of regret, where Iain was. But she knew one thing.

That email wasn't from Sarah MacKenzie.

Maggie had seen a lot in the last year. A lot of things she never would have believed before she'd arrived in Scotland. But even she had her limits. Ghosts may be real, but she was pretty sure

they didn't use email. That meant someone—someone *alive*—
wanted her to think they did. And that gave Maggie a place to start.

Sarah MacKenzie.

Or more precisely, Sarah MacKenzie's flat.

* * *

"I want to see that flat," Benson declared as she settled into
one of the chairs opposite Warwick's desk. They had agreed to meet
first thing that morning to discuss next steps in the investigation.
Benson had brought the donuts.

Warwick considered her day. She'd already overplanned it
with follow-up on half a dozen cases. She might as well add one
more thing. Especially since she'd made some room in her schedule
by convincing Cameron to let her dump the grave-robbing case
onto Willis now, now that she'd taken on both the assist on
Benson's Edinburgh homicide and the newly reopened
investigation of Sarah MacKenzie's suicide.

"Good idea," Warwick replied to Benson as she sipped
coffee from a styrofoam cup. That had been her contribution to the
breakfast, straight from the precinct's lunchroom. "I need be back
here by two o'clock. I'll be handing off the grave-robbing case to
another sergeant, and he doesn't come on until then. He'll need a
specific and slow briefing." She sighed. "With time for questions."

Benson offered an intrigued smile and was about to ask for
more information when Warwick's phone rang.

Warwick picked up the receiver. "Elizabeth Warwick. Yes.
No, I hadn't heard. Yes, it's still my case, at least for a few more
hours. No, no trouble. It's my job. Yes, I'll be out right away. Thank
you."

She hung up. "Change of plan," she announced. "We'll have
to visit the flat after I meet with Sergeant Willis. There's been
another one."

"Another murder?"

Warwick shook her head. "Another grave robbery."

* * *

The city of Aberdeen began as two distinct settlements: Old Aberdeen at the mouth of the river Don, and New Aberdeen, a fishing and trading village on the Denburn waterway. The towns merged under a single city charter granted by William the Lion in 1179 and quickly became a trading and commercial center of Northern Scotland. In the ensuing centuries, between booms and busts, ravaged by wars against the English and raids by rival Scottish lords, the city continued to expand in all directions, absorbing suburbs to the north, west, and south, until finally it reached its current borders, covering over seventy square miles of neighborhoods and green spaces sweeping back beautifully from the icy waters of the North Sea.

At the very outermost reaches of the city, in the western district of Cults, stood a small clapboard church, mostly forgotten except for handful of local faithful who eschewed the larger and more ornate offerings downtown for the simplicity and convenience of somewhat run-down, but Protestantly bare little church.

The church had been founded after some of the more tumultuous periods of Scottish history and thus had avoided the whiplash-like denominational changes imposed on older houses of worship by succeeding victors. It was small and Presbyterian, always had been, and hosted a matching small and Presbyterian graveyard, notable for no reason save one particular occupant.

Warwick pulled her car over to the side of the road and parked directly across from the church. It was all white with a simple wooden cross atop a not-terribly-tall steeple.

"Not much to look at," Benson commented.

Warwick just shrugged. She wasn't going to judge a house

of worship. "The cemetery must be around back," she said as she unfastened her seatbelt and opened the car door. "Let's see if they're waiting for us inside the church or in the cemetery."

A quick circuit around the building confirmed the callers were out back in the graveyard. The defiled grave was impossible to miss. Even if the two trained detectives hadn't noticed the enormous pile of dirt next to the gaping, coffin-sized hole in the ground, they would have noticed the two white-haired women standing next to the headstone, wringing their hands and looking relieved to finally have someone official upon whom to unburden their story.

"Oh, thank God you've come," said the shorter and stouter of the two.

"*Finally* come," added the taller, thinner woman. She wore thick, round glasses.

"Aye," agreed the first woman. "Thank God you've finally come. It's a terrible business."

"A tragic business."

"Aye, a terrible, tragic business." The shorter woman nodded up to her counterpart. "We discovered it this morning."

"Early this morning."

"Aye, we discovered it early this morning. We didn't know what to do, so we called you."

"Called you right away."

"Aye, right away we called you. Right away. And now here you are."

"Finally," finished the taller woman.

It seemed like a pause, so Warwick jumped in, even if only to stop what the two had likely long ago failed to realize was an astonishingly annoying speech pattern. "Yes, here we are."

First she introduced herself and Benson. Then she got their

names: Miriam and Muriel. Miriam was the stout chatterer; Muriel the lanky corrector. Then, having ascertained their identities, Warwick separated them. Muriel was sent inside to pull the records on the grave. Miriam remained outside to tell the full story, uninterrupted.

"We came in early this morning," Miriam started. "Like every morning. Not especially early. Not earlier than normal, I mean. Just regular early."

Warwick began to appreciate the value of a Muriel to keep Miriam focused. She nodded to show she'd gotten the point. "Go on."

"Aye, well, it's not like we walk the grounds every morning. In fact, we rarely do. There's more than enough to do inside the church, there is. But Muriel came out onto the back porch to shake out the rugs—that's her job, you see. I'm allergic to dust. Always have been. Pollen too. Which you'd think would always be the case—being allergic to both that is, since they would seem so similar—but actually it's quite common to be allergic to only one and not the other. It's two entirely different types of allergies, it is. Pollen is plant matter, but if you're allergic to dust, then really you're allergic to the dust mites in the dust, and of course they're animals. Small animals, to be sure, but—"

"Miriam?" Benson interrupted just before Warwick did. "What did Muriel see when she shook out the rugs?"

Miriam nodded. "Oh, aye, right. Well, of course, she saw this."

Miriam waved at the open grave and its attendant pile of earth. A quick glance to the church confirmed it would have been quite visible, and conspicuous, from the back door.

"Then what happened?" Warwick asked.

"Aye, well, Muriel screamed, didn't she? I came running

from where I'd been cleaning the altar. You've no idea how dirty the inside of a church can get, even during the week. Oh, sure, you'd expect it on a Sunday, what with everyone rushing in and kicking everything up and leaving again, but just a random Thursday can leave an unbelievable amount of dust behind. Did I mention I'm allergic to dust? Actually, I'm allergic to the dust mites in the du—"

"Miriam?" Warwick interrupted. "What did you do when you heard Muriel scream?"

Miriam nodded again. She seemed accustomed to being interrupted and put back on task. Muriel was seeming considerably less rude than she had at first blush.

"Well," said Miriam, "I ran over to see what the matter was. And when I saw—well, you can hardly miss it, can you?—when I saw, well then, I screamed too, didn't I?"

Warwick suppressed a frown at the thought of these two women screaming at a pile of dirt. She considered that the two detectives investigating were also women, and decided to chalk it up to the church-ladies' generation rather than gender. She peered into the grave herself. It looked much the same as the one at the Aberdeen Municipal Cemetery. The coffin was a darker wood, and it didn't appear to have the two-part lid, but otherwise it was covered in the same pattern of loose dirt and criss-crossed shovel marks.

"Did either of you go down into the grave?" Benson asked.

Miriam gasped and clutched her throat. "Oh, dear Lord, no! Oh, no, of course not. No, no. We hurried over and took a quick look, didn't we? But then it was straight back inside to call you folk."

Warwick frowned into the grave. "Why were you waiting for us out here then?"

Warwick didn't suspect them. She needed to know what they might have done to contaminate the scene.

Miriam looked puzzled. Well, more puzzled than usual. "This is where the grave is," she explained simply.

Warwick shrugged. That was the right answer, she supposed. Before she could delve into where exactly she and her fellow caretaker had trod, Muriel came shuffling back out of the church, a raft of papers in her hand. Too many papers, it seemed to Warwick.

"I've found the records," Muriel announced as she reached them, "but the grave is too old and the handwriting is too small. I can't tell what goes to what, so I brought all the cemetery records for you. Here."

She shoved the papers at the detectives. After a moment of hesitation, occasioned by the largesse of the records, Benson accepted them.

"Thank you," Warwick said. "We'll review them back at the station." She didn't want to pour over them just then, especially if they were, as they appeared, well out of order and filled with small script from centuries earlier. She pointed at the headstone. "Do you know anything about the person who was buried here?"

They all looked at the headstone. Muriel read it aloud. "Eileen NicInnes Jenkins. Born 1798. Died 1844."

"Does that name ring any bells?" Warwick asked.

The women just looked at the name etched into the stone, both their faces twisted into expressions of consideration.

"Can you think of any reason," Benson added, "why this particular grave was disturbed?"

Muriel shrugged, but Miriam's face slowly lit with recognition. "I know the name," she said. "I think. I mean, I couldn't be sure without looking at the records. But yes..." She glanced around at the small graveyard and nodded. "Yes, I think that's right."

"What is?" Warwick asked. "What's right?"

Miriam nodded some more. She gestured to the area they were standing in. "Do you see where we are now? This is the section closest to the church. This was the original cemetery for the founders of the church and their families."

"Was Eileen Jenkins one of the founders of the church?"

Miriam squinted at the headstone. "Oh, no. Eileen wouldn't have been but a babe then. But her mother, her mother came here shortly after the church opened. I didn't recognize the last name at first, but her mother... Oh, most of us in the congregation know the story of her mother."

Benson cocked her head. "Why is that?"

A fair question, Warwick thought. She had a more practical one. "Is her mother buried here too?"

"Oh, no," Miriam answered quickly. "Her mother isn't buried here. She was excommunicated."

Warwick frowned. "Excommunicated? Isn't that a Catholic practice? I thought this was a Presbyterian church."

"Aye, it is," Miriam agreed. "What I mean is, she and her babe came to this church *because* she was excommunicated. And it was on account of *why* she was excommunicated that the church elders decided not to bury her on the grounds here."

"Why was she excommunicated?" Benson asked. Warwick had already guessed the answer.

"For arcane practices," Miriam said.

"For being a witch," Muriel clarified.

"Aye," Miriam sighed. "For being a witch."

* * *

Which, which, which, Maggie considered as she neared the

destination of her stroll: the campus. She was trying to decide which coffee shop to spend her afternoon in. She was fully prepared for her visit to Sarah MacKenzie's flat. Well, almost fully prepared. She would have preferred to have had her Dark Book with her. But that notwithstanding, she was ready. She knew the address; she knew what she wanted to find out; and she knew the most important thing of all: to wait until nightfall.

There was no way she was breaking and entering in broad daylight.

Which, she ruminated, meant an afternoon in a coffee shop on campus, followed by dinner at her favorite campus pub, before walking quietly and unnoticed—she hoped—to Sarah's college district flat.

Then she spied it. The Green Door Cafe, with its very much white door, thank you. A place she'd first gone to with Sarah MacKenzie. Maggie smiled as she realized she hadn't selected her route to campus as much as she'd it allowed it to select her, not unlike her foggy walk from the train station upon her arrival from Edinburgh. She took it as an omen. Where it began, it might also end. When one door closes, another opens. Or something like that.

And sometimes, Maggie thought as she grabbed ahold of The Green Door's white door, *you have to open your own doors.*

* * *

"Should we open it?" Benson craned her neck to peer into the witch's grave. Or rather, the witch's daughter's grave.

Warwick glanced down as well. She shook her head. "No. Let's wait for forensics to process the scene. They can open it up and see what's missing."

"Missing? How do you know something's missing?" Muriel asked with more than a little disgust in her voice. Miriam just listened to the question, then nodded at the sergeant, wide-eyed, joining her friend's question.

"It's my job to know," Warwick answered.

It was an impressive response, and her decision to allow the forensics officers to open the casket, a professional one. But she also hadn't quite shaken the odor of Jenny Burns' casket. This grave was older and she had already detected the stench seeping up from the coffin below. Warwick was usually hands-on, but she knew sometimes it was better to let someone else open the box.

Just ask Pandora.

15. Evening Constitutional

Maggie looked at the clock on the café wall. It was time for her to go for her walk. The sun had set and a cool mist was descending onto the twilight streets. She had her backpack and everything she needed. She took the last sip of her last cup of tea and headed out into the darkening night.

* * *

Iain glanced down at his watch. He needed to go for a walk. His companion had left and unbidden thoughts were flooding his mind. He had everything he needed and nothing he wanted. He craved the first drink of the night but instead headed out into the darkening night.

* * *

Philip checked the clock on his desk. He decided to go for a walk. His research was complete and a dull fatigue clouded his thoughts. He had ideas in his head and a plan in mind. He took a parting drink from his water bottle and headed out into the darkening night.

* * *

Warwick peered up at the clock on her wall. She wanted to go for a walk. The grave-robbing case was delegated to Willis and her concentration was focused on her newest case. She took another drink of coffee from her Styrofoam cup and headed out into the darkening night.

* * *

Sinclair neither knew nor cared what time it was. And he had no plans to go anywhere. He was confident that, in time, others would come to him.

16. Apartment Hunting

Autumn had definitely arrived. Summer was a short season at the 58th parallel, especially on the top half of an island sticking into the North Sea. The day had been warm enough, but the sun had set a few minutes earlier than the previous day and a thin fog rolled in from the harbor to coat the streets. It surrounded Maggie's ankles as she glided beneath the streetlights on her way to Sarah MacKenzie's flat.

The flat was located one block off the main street of one of the more eclectic neighborhoods straddling the border between the college and the rest of Aberdeen proper. It was a three-story building with small balconies facing the street. The front door was secured, with a tiny lobby visible through the glass and an intercom system on the outside wall. The intercom was a silver-colored metal plate with a dozen push buttons and a circle-shaped series of slats for staticky and unintelligible conversation. Maggie examined the buttons, or rather, the names on the labels stuck next to them. She didn't know whether Sarah's name would still be there. If not, she could guess the one blank button was hers. She supposed it might be difficult to rent an apartment where someone had killed herself.

The labels proved less than helpful, however. Trendy neighborhood or not, the landlord was not keeping up appearances—at least not in terms of keeping the intercom updated. Three of the buttons had no labels, and the labels that were there seemed old and likely out-of-date.

Maggie frowned. She was sticking with her empty-apartment-because-somebody-died-inside theory. It was part logic, part wishful thinking. If it had been rented out already, the new tenants would probably resist her efforts to snoop around their home. Either way, the directory was unhelpful, so she had to go to Plan B.

She just wished she knew what Plan B was.

Actually, she knew what Plan B was; she just wished it were something better. She shrugged and stepped off the porch to look up at the flats. There were six facing the street, which, combined with the twelve intercom buttons, suggested six more facing the back. She scanned the area and spied a gate, guarding a narrow walkway along the side of the building.

She stiffened a bit as a car drove past, on its way to the main street, which was uncomfortably near and busy. She watched as it turned off the side street, then looked up again at the apartment building. Four of the flats had lights on just then. That left two in the front which might be empty—and therefore might have been Sarah's. She made a mental note of that, then headed for the gate.

She hoped to find at least one other lightless flat in the back. If she was going to have to do what she was starting to think she might have to do, she was going to want some privacy—or at least more privacy than afforded out front with its lights and traffic.

The gate wasn't locked. It was wrought iron bars, about as tall as her, and easily swung open after she reached through and undid the latch. The pathway was paved with large flagstones. She looked down to watch every step, since there was no lighting just there and she'd had bad luck walking across uneven stones in the dark. A few moments later, she was standing in a tiny courtyard behind the building, paved with smaller red bricks. She stood as far back as she could and looked up at the balconies. Five of the six had lights on. So she had selected her target. That was the good news. The bad news was that the unlit flat was on the top floor.

Of course, she sighed. She'd have to hope the remaining five tenants wouldn't be looking out their balcony windows just then. Maybe there was a football match on. Celtic versus Rangers would be the best, if she recalled Iain's explanation of Scottish soccer loyalties correctly.

Iain.

She sighed again.

Stupid Iain. He should have been waiting out front for her, ignorant and worried, but supportive nonetheless. What she wouldn't have given for an ignorant and supportive boyfriend just then. And cute. Ignorant, supportive, and cute.

A third sigh. There was nothing wrong with a wistful pause, but she had work to do, by herself if necessary. She looked up at the one dark balcony. There was no scaffolding or ladder to climb up. She'd expected as much.

She'd managed not to use the magic since the nightmare on the train. Although she didn't recall it, she knew the dream meant she'd used the magic shortly before—during The Lost Weeks. She'd avoided it since, afraid of what she might have done during those weeks to have resulted in both inexplicable amnesia and tortuous nightmares.

But she wasn't scared of another nightmare. Not any more. Now she was scared she wouldn't have any more nightmares. She was scared the magic was gone. The Dark Book was gone. Iain was gone. Maybe the magic was gone too. And despite her usual rationality—or perhaps because of it—she had decided not to test it.

She knew it was better to fear the magic was gone forever, than to fail at it and confirm its loss.

But her respite was over. Time for the test.

The first spell she'd ever tried was also the first one that had ever worked. It hadn't worked the first time. Not the second time either. But eventually, after enough tries, and after learning enough to make her think the magic might actually be real, it had worked. A simple spell. Basic, really.

Levitation.

There was a certain poetry to that being the first spell she had mastered. It wasn't just the simplicity of it, but its perfection as a symbol of how the magic worked. For the magic in the Dark Book was dark magic, and levitation, as benign as it might seem, actually illustrated exactly how the dark magic worked. The dark magic attacked and destroyed the natural order of things.

Things don't levitate. They fall. Rocks fall. Leaves fall. Apples fall. They fall on the heads of brilliant physicists who realize that apples always fall. *Always*. And that was a law that couldn't be broken.

Except by the dark magic.

Maggie looked down and spied a small rock laying loosely atop the uneven bricks of the courtyard.

Even the words of the spell confirmed its counter-natural power: 'Tear asunder the bonds which chain this object to the Earth.'

She whispered the well-learned spell in its original tongue, "*Mhaidhid inh chuimriachan anh-í chonrig riátsha cho inh Thalum,*" and waited. Nothing happened at first and Maggie felt a bolt of panic strike her heart. But rather than repeat the spell, she simply concentrated on the pebble, the words she had just whispered echoing in her mind.

After a moment, or maybe two, the pebble stirred, almost imperceptibly. Maggie allowed herself a deep exhale of relief. She hadn't even realized she was holding her breath. She narrowed her eyes and repeated the spell.

"*Mhaidhid inh chuimriachan anh-í chonrig riátsha cho inh Thalum.*"

This time, the pebble floated straight up, accelerating as it went. Maggie had expected it to stop at her eye level, but it glided up and shot out of sight into the darkness above her.

Good to know, she thought. *Pay attention to the distance.*

If she was going to levitate herself up to the balcony—and she was—she didn't want to accidentally end up in the stratosphere. She glanced around. No one appeared to be watching her. No one had come out onto their balcony. *Go Celtic. Or Rangers. Or whoever.* She closed her eyes and imagined herself being raised weightless to the top of the balcony. She didn't just imagine. She remembered. And it felt good.

"*Mhaidhid inh chuimriachan anh-í chonrig riátsha cho inh Thalum.*"

A feeling of utter weightless came over her and she opened her eyes. She didn't feel like she was rising. That would have involved noticing herself traveling against the force of gravity. Instead, she felt separated from it as the building scrolled past her like the pan of a camera.

The feeling of the magic—not the effect on her body as on object of it, but the power of wielding it—was instantly intoxicating. It had been too long and the force of it almost distracted her from her goal: the balcony. And the danger: the stratosphere. At the last moment, she extended a dreamlike hand and grabbed the balcony railing. The reconnection to the real world—the world bound by gravity, the world that only worked *because* of gravity, whose foundations and pillars and beams and bricks and mortar and nails relied on the constant, relentless, inescapable downward pull of gravity to keep the building together—this connection ripped Maggie from her state of weightlessness and she could feel the spell slough off of her like melting snow from a tree branch. She quickly pulled herself toward the building and landed safely on the floor of the balcony as the last of the levitation spell vanished from her.

She waited a few moments, crouched on hand and knee, to see whether any of the neighbors had torn their eyes from the undoubtedly riveting nil-nil tie to catch a glimpse of the flying American girl. A few more moments without so much as a, 'Did you see that, love?' and Maggie felt comfortable that her unorthodox ascent had gone undetected.

She stood up and appraised the balcony's sliding glass door. She guessed she wasn't done with the magic. She grabbed the handle and tugged. Sure enough, it was locked.

Damn.

This particular obstacle brought into crystalline focus just how dire the loss of the Dark Book truly was. She had memorized the levitation spell, but there were scores of spells between the intricate leather covers of her Dark Book. She hadn't memorized all of them. She'd barely translated some of them. Undoubtedly, there was something in there about getting through locked doors. The need to get through a locked door was as old as the first door lock. But without the Book, Maggie had no real idea where to begin. Levitation was unlikely to do it. The other spells she could do without referring to the Book seemed equally unlikely to help: igniting things; diving information. The only one that seemed even potentially helpful was the transmutation spell. If she could turn the glass into paper... But that spell was hard. And complicated. Even with the Book cracked open in front of her, she'd had little success with it.

No, she couldn't get in with magic alone. Not the dark magic anyway. She couldn't fight the laws of nature to get the result she wanted. But maybe, she realized, she could embrace those laws.

The door was glass. Glass breaks.

She pulled off her shoe and slammed it against the glass nearest the door handle. It bounced right off again, barely leaving a mark. She looked at the soft sole of her thin shoe, unjustifiably surprised that something so small and flimsy had failed to shatter tempered glass. A scan of the balcony revealed no objects strong enough to break the door. No metal deck chairs or anything. In fact, there was nothing at all, just an empty, slightly dusty balcony. Looking on the bright side, the lack of furnishings suggested she likely had the correct flat. She looked over the edge of the balcony at the brick patio below.

That'll do, she thought.

This would be different. The same spell, but used, not to send something away, but rather to bring something to her. She selected a brick directly below her that seemed to have a wider gap on one side, and repeated the levitation spell.

The brick shuddered against its neighbors, but Maggie kept her concentration on the object and willed it upward. There was no need for her to say the spell again. The brick was coming; it just needed a moment to scrape past its surrounding bricks. The force necessary to do that was sizeable so when it finally did break free, the brick shot upward at a surprising rate, and Maggie had to react quickly to snatch it out of the air as it flew by.

The impact stung her hand, but she shook it off as she turned to face the balcony door, reminded yet again that there was no healing spell.

Simply tossing the brick through the pane was one option,

but she wasn't convinced it might not just bounce off and smash her in the face. Also, she couldn't imagine anything making more noise than that—certainly enough to pull at least one neighbor away from the tele. She needed to be quieter than that; she didn't want to hurry once she was inside, worried that the neighbors had called the cops. She'd read stories where the heroes break into some top secret facility, tripping all the alarms and security measures, but not caring because they knew it would take the guards four minutes to arrive but they only needed three to grab the goods and get out. That wasn't Maggie. She'd left her ninja outfit at home. This wasn't smash and grab; it was enter and explore. She needed time, which meant she needed quiet. She wasn't sure how long it might take Aberdeen's finest to arrive after a neighbor called the police to report the sound of breaking glass on the balcony above, but she didn't want to find out either.

Holding the brick like a hammer, she struck the glass right by the door handle. And as she did so, the glass shattering from the force, she cast the levitation spell on the exploding shards. She captured all but one of them, holding them weightless, and silent, in the air as one lone shard crashed and tinkled on the balcony floor. She would have preferred no noise, but it was quiet enough. She decided it was unlikely to evoke the suspicions of the other apartment dwellers.

She carefully lowered the remainder of the broken glass to the cement, the pieces clinking only slightly as they settled. Then she reached through the broken pane and unlocked the door.

She was in.

With a new appreciation for the accuracy of the term 'breaking and entering.'

Any lingering doubts that she might have chosen the wrong flat were dispelled once she stepped inside. It was deserted. There was no furniture, and the pungent smell of fresh paint and new carpet almost, but not quite, masked a different, unpleasant smell. Maggie could guess what that was, recalling the news story that it had taken several days for the body to be found.

A part of her was glad for the clean up job. She wasn't particularly interested in exploring a gory death scene. On the other hand, she was disheartened somewhat because she knew her chances of discovering something useful had been greatly diminished by the landlord's attempts to scrub the space clean of the tragedy that had occurred there.

She extracted a flashlight from her backpack and swept its beam across the flat. The news report said Sarah had hanged herself over a closet door. There was a front hall closet, but she decided to check the bedroom. There was something eerily intimate about taking one's own life. It seemed like the sort of thing one would do in private—more bedroom than foyer. It was just a feeling, but she had learned to trust her feelings.

She pointed the flashlight downward and walked silently across the new carpet to the larger of two bedrooms. It was Sarah's bedroom. Maggie just knew it somehow. She'd never been there, but she knew it. There was a feeling in the room. Almost a presence. And for the first time it occurred to her that, although it was unlikely that Sarah's ghost had sent her the email, it was not at all unlikely that Sarah's ghost was still around, and specifically, still in the very apartment where Maggie found herself.

A chill ran up her spine. She wondered whether it was just the thought of the ghost or maybe the ghost itself. She'd heard that people who reported seeing ghosts often described a sudden drop in temperature or a cool spot in the room.

Maggie stood up straight and closed her eyes. She took a deep breath. *Calm down, Devereaux*, she told herself. *Don't freak yourself out.*

When she opened her eyes, everything seemed normal and distinctly un-ghostlike again. Dark, empty, maybe even sad, but not obviously haunted. Nevertheless, she began to feel an urgency to get done and get out. The neighbors may not have called the police over a single piece of glass breaking, but that didn't mean she had to dawdle. She knew ghosts could be benign, but she didn't know if Sarah's would be, given how they'd last parted ways. She hurried to the bedroom's closet door and opened it.

It was solid wood, not the hollow-core kind, and on sturdy hinges. A good choice, she had to admit. She inspected the door knob, guessing Sarah had likely tied one end of the rope to the inside knob before stretching it over the top and around her neck.

Maggie shook her head at the thought. She hadn't known Sarah that well, but she never thought she'd harm herself like that. She seemed too strong, too determined. But then, isn't that what people always said about the person who committed suicide? They never saw it coming.

Maggie noticed the outside of the door had a fresh coat of still shiny paint, but the interior seemed to have missed the make over. A swing of the flashlight beam confirmed an older, duller, yellower paint inside the closet, with years' worth of smudges and stains still visible. There was a single bar for coat hangers beneath a single shelf that was a little too tall to be comfortably used. More for storage, it seemed, than everyday items like scarves and hats.

She glanced around for something, anything that might have remained from before the paint brushes arrived. But she spied nothing on the floor of the closet or the bedroom. Just clean, new, wall-to-wall carpet.

Her intent had been to find some object Sarah had touched and cast the diving spell. She hoped that would give her a clue about the suicide and how it related to the disappearance of her Dark Book. The only thing she could think of trying was the doorknob, but she doubted that would work. How many people had touched that doorknob since Sarah's body was found? How many cops and paramedics? How many landlords and painters and carpet installers? No, she needed something personal. Something all those people had overlooked.

She glanced up again at the too-high closet shelf. She couldn't see what was up on it. And she realized neither could the cops and paramedics and landlords.

With no furniture to stand on, Maggie uttered the levitation spell a third time and lifted herself off the carpet. She knew she was going to pay a price for directing the magic on herself so much—the nightmares were always worse when she performed the magic on herself—but she wasn't sure what choice she had. The feeling in her stomach telling her to hurry up was getting stronger. She needed to find something before the feeling became overwhelming and she fled empty-handed, a burglar without her loot.

Her tenacity paid off. Up on the shelf, shoved into a back corner, just out of reach of the swipes in the dust from a half-hearted cleaning attempt, was a very small and very broken picture frame. She plucked it from the shelf and allowed herself to drop again to the carpet.

She turned the frame over in her hands. It was only big enough for a wallet-sized photo, and the photo was long gone. One corner had been completely smashed, leaving it hanging open like an incomplete rectangle, and the glass that had once covered whatever photo was inside was missing save a few broken shards jutting out from where they were trapped in the wooden edges. It looked like it had been punched or thrown against the wall during an argument or fit—just the sort of thing that might have left strong emotional information behind. Maybe the subject of the missing photo was the cause of Sarah's grief. Maybe she smashed it to pieces shortly before deciding to end it all. She'd thrown the glass and photo in the trash can and tossed the frame out of the way, up on the storage shelf. It was worth a try. Maggie set the frame down on the carpet and prepared to cast the diving spell.

Then she heard something.

She was focused enough on the picture frame, that she wasn't exactly sure what she heard. A footstep? A door latch? A floorboard squeaking? A neighbor? The police? Sarah's ghost?

She wasn't going to wait around to find out.

She stuffed the frame into her backpack and crept quickly out of the bedroom—flashlight extinguished, back to the wall, eyes darting in the dark. There was no one in the living room.

Or at least, she couldn't *see* anyone in the living room.

She faced a Hobson's choice. If it was the police or a neighbor, they were likely coming in through the front door, unless they knew the levitation spell too. So if she went out that way, she'd walk right into their grasp. On the other hand, if she went out the balcony, the only way down—safely—was with the magic. As difficult as it might be to explain to the police what she was doing walking out of the late Sarah MacKenzie's flat, it would be infinitely more difficult to explain what she was doing floating down from it.

She decided to take her chances with the front door. She'd talked her way out of a lot in her life. The trick was limiting what she had to explain. She crossed over to the front door and peered through the peephole. There didn't appear to be anyone in the hallway. *Good.* She turned the knob and opened the door ever so slightly. No one grabbed the door and yanked it open. *Also good.* She pushed it all the way open. There was, in fact, no one there. *All good.*

Then she thought she heard the same noise again, from inside the flat. She bolted down the hallway and straight for the stairs, not even caring that she'd left the apartment door to slam shut behind her. She hit the stairwell at a full run and dashed down the stairs two at a time. The stairwell ended at a door to the lobby. She darted through the small foyer and out the front door as fast as she could, looking back over her shoulder as she broke the plane of the exit to see if anyone was following her.

She ran right into the person standing on the sidewalk in front of the apartment building.

Maggie tumbled to the ground, landing on the wet grass next to the walkway between the building and the street. She straightened her glasses and looked up, completely stunned to see the person whose presence had sent her sprawling to the ground.

"What are *you* doing here?" she gasped.

17. Fancy Meeting You Here

"Hello, Maggie," Elizabeth Warwick greeted the dumbstruck American student sprawled at her feet.

Maggie didn't reply immediately. She was still trying to figure out what the hell she had just gotten herself into. And how the hell to get herself out of it.

"Maggie?" asked another woman towering over her. "Maggie Despereuax?"

"Devereaux," Maggie corrected as she finally pulled herself to her feet. The grass was wet. Now her butt was too, which was both irritating and distracting. "Do I know you?" she asked the second woman.

Benson didn't reply to the question. Instead, she confirmed, "The American niece. The one with the missing—"

"Yes," Warwick interrupted sharply. "The American niece."

"Missing what?" Maggie asked. She didn't like that they knew things about her. She liked it even less that Sgt. Warwick was trying to hide what they knew.

"The missing piece of the puzzle," Warwick asserted, rather lamely, Maggie thought. "Maybe." Then Warwick changed the subject. "What are you doing here, Maggie?"

Maggie assessed the situation. She still didn't know who the other woman was, although it was pretty obvious she was a cop too. They knew something about her. They knew something was missing.

Did they know about the Dark Book?!

She thought no one knew about the book. Except Sinclair. And Iain. Oh, and Sarah. But Sarah was dead.

And Maggie had just been caught right outside the dead woman's flat by two police officers. Yep. That pretty much summed up the situation.

Deflectors to full force, Commander Devereaux.

She crossed her arms and looked at Warwick. "I could ask you the same question."

Warwick grinned and shook her head, seemingly amused by the response.

Benson not so much. "We're the police."

"Exactly." Maggie pointed at her. "And I pay your salary."

Benson hesitated for a moment, taken aback. "No, you don't. You're not British. You don't pay taxes here. And certainly not in Edinburgh."

Edinburgh? Maggie tried not to panic. This cop was from Edinburgh? As in, dead-man-in-the-bathtub Edinburgh? *Oh, bad, bad, bad.*

Warwick pointed to the flats. "Did you know Sarah MacKenzie?"

Maggie froze. She considered her options. If she said no, she might get caught in the lie later. Maybe. If she said yes, they would know it was no accident she was standing outside her dead ex-professor's flat. She decided to go with later and maybe.

"No."

Warwick frowned and crossed her arms. "You know we can check the records, right, Maggie?"

Not right now, you can't, thought Maggie.

"Yeah, well," Maggie stammered, "it's a big university. I might be mistaken."

Maggie smiled inside. That would give her just enough wiggle room for the later and the maybe. 'Oh, *that* Sarah MacKenzie. My faculty advisor. Right. Okay. Sure. I knew *her*.'

"She's dead, Maggie," Warwick announced evenly. "Do you know anything about that?"

Maggie stood up straight. "I can honestly say, I don't know anything about her death."

Despite my best efforts just now.

"What about a murder in Edinburgh last month?" Benson asked. "Where a witness saw a Canadian—or perhaps American—woman fleeing the scene?"

Maggie didn't have a reply ready for that question. "Ehh..." she started, wishing she hadn't.

"I think," Warwick said, "we're going to have to ask you to come with us down to the—"

"Maggie!"

Everyone turned toward the male voice that had just called out. It was Philip. He was rushing over from the main road.

"There you are," he said as he reached their gathering. "I'm so sorry. I guess I took a wrong turn. You must have been looking everywhere for me."

Maggie couldn't help but smile. She appreciated his skill at prevarication. It was good to be with someone like her. "Uh, yeah. I was looking everywhere. For you."

"Well, here I am." Philip threw his arms wide. "Let's get back to our evening, shall we?"

Maggie looked at the police officers to see if they might block her departure. They didn't.

"Enjoy your evening," Warwick said with a curt nod. "We'll talk again."

Benson said nothing, apparently deferring to her host.

Maggie didn't waste the opportunity. She stuck her arm through Philip's and they hurried away from Sarah MacKenzie's flat, and the cops.

"Thanks, Philip," Maggie whispered even though they had made it out of earshot. "You're a life saver."

Philip shrugged. "Glad to help. Now you owe me one."

She looked up at him, unsure what he meant by that, but he smiled.

"Fancy a pint, me lass?" he said in a terrible attempt at a Scottish accent. "I've a wee bit of a business proposition for ye, I do."

Maggie returned his smile. "Aye, me laddy. Lead the way. I'm all ears."

18. Yes, Mama

The nightmare started the same way the evening had ended: Maggie walking arm-in-arm with Philip down a bright, vibrant street. Kicking through the low fog, and gliding from pool to pool of light cast by the streetlamps. The night felt weightless.

But then they turned down a dimmer street. The fog was thicker at her feet. She was holding hands with Iain now. She looked up at him. He offered a tight smile—pained, disappointed—but didn't say anything, and looked away. The lightness in heart tightened.

The fog was growing denser. It pushed against the weakening light of the farther spaced streetlamps. Her father walked next to her, his arm around her shoulder, but his gaze cast away. She knew something was wrong. Her father was dead, wasn't he? No, he was still alive. It was her mother. Her mother was dead.

And her mother was walking next to her, marching briskly forward, Maggie hurrying to keep up, her hands clutched desperately to her mother's purse straps.

It started to rain.

"Try to keep up, Maggie," he mother scolded. "We don't want to get caught out in the cold."

She grabbed Maggie's arm and yanked her into a sheltered

alcove under a stone bridgeway. It was a dead end, but there were two doors in the wall, one white and one black. The wind blew a spray of icy rain against their backs.

"Which door, mama?" Maggie asked. She wished her mother would look at her. She was having trouble remembering what she looked like.

But her mother kept her back to her as she examined the doors. "The white one. The white one, or none at all."

Maggie nodded. "Yes, mama." *Of course, mama.*

Her mother grabbed ahold of the white door's handle and pulled. It didn't open. She tugged several more times, wrenching the handle, but the deadbolt just clanked against the stone doorframe.

"Is it locked, mama?"

"Hush, Maggie," her mother hissed.

"Yes, mama." *Of course, mama.*

Her mother grabbed the handle again with both hands. She exhaled deeply, then muttered something under her breath and yanked again, as hard as she could.

The handle broke off the door completely, cracking the wood and bringing a chuck of door with it. Maggie's mother threw the twisted mechanism against the wet cobblestones.

"Good job, mama!" Maggie squealed.

Her mother half turned to her. A faint smile was visible, but Maggie still couldn't see her whole face. Her mother turned again and pulled the white door open by the broken hole where the handle and lock had been.

But the entrance was walled shut. Floor to ceiling, thick red bricks with dried mortar sealed the entry. They'd never get inside.

Maggie's mother slammed a fist against the brick wall and lowered her head against the back of her hand. There was no noise, save the howl of the wind, but Maggie could see her mother's shoulders shake in deep sobs.

What about the black door? Maggie thought. But she didn't dare ask that.

"Are you all right, Mama?"

Her mother didn't answer. Not at first. Her back heaved a few more times, then she wiped her eyes and finally turned around to face her daughter.

Maggie frowned. She didn't recognize her face. She didn't know what her mother even looked like.

She grabbed Maggie's arm and jerked her deeper into the alcove. "Come with me."

Maggie didn't even think to resist. She watched the black door pass her by as she was pulled out of the rain and into the silence of a hitherto unnoticed corner of their stone shelter.

"I'm tired, Maggie," her mother said. She laid down on a long stone bench, then gestured toward an identical bench next to her. It was marble, bleached white, and looked very, very cold. "Lay down next to me."

Maggie hesitated.

"Please, Maggie. I have to lay down. Lay down too."

Maggie stood frozen.

"Lay down!" her mother barked.

Maggie nodded quickly. She fought off the defiance growing in her heart. "Yes, mama." *Of course, mama.*

Then she laid down inside the stone casket next to her mother's sealed sarcophagus.

Maggie could still see the sky. The roof of the alcove was gone. Dark clouds rushed by in the gray firmament. The stone was cold against her back.

She wanted to cry.

She refused to let herself.

She watched, dry-eyed, as the stone lid scraped across her coffin and sealed her in. She could hear the shovelfuls of dirt hitting the lid.

Thump.

Thump.

Thump.

She pounded against the lid. She screamed for help. But no one came.

Not Philip.

Not Iain.

Not her father.

And certainly not her mother.

"It's too late, Maggie," she heard her mother's voice. "It's too late."

Maggie stopped pounding and screaming.

"Yes, mama. Of course, mama."

Maggie rolled over in her bed, ascending out of the dream like a bubble rising slowly to the surface of the water. Then she pulled the covers against her face and finally let herself cry.

19. The Witch Bone Is Connected to...

It was like a puzzle. Putting the pieces together. Except it wasn't like a puzzle. There was nothing to solve. The pieces went where the pieces went. The mystery wasn't in the putting together of the bones. The mystery was in the bones themselves. And the solution was in extracting it.

The hand bone connected to the arm bone...

Frankenstein's monster was coming along nicely. But there was more work to be done.

20. Picking a Destination

Maggie turned the picture frame over and over in her hands. Her morning coffee was cooling to just the right temperature and the bright sun rising outside belied the cooler autumn day it was bringing. The peacefulness of the morning gave her a chance to contemplate both the object in her hand and Philip's 'business' proposition.

The business position was actually an invitation to the conference Hamilton was speaking at. The university had already paid for Sarah to attend, so he was allowed to go in her stead. It was being held October 31-November 1 on the Isle of Lewis, near the world-famous Callanish standing stones. He'd given her the conference brochure as he explained the arrangement, but she had completely tuned him out when she flipped through and came across the description of the stones:

Dating back over 4000 years, the Callanish standing stones are second in importance only to Stonehenge. The heart is a central circle of 13 tall stones where excavations uncovered a chambered tomb reported to have contained human remains. From there four limbs run out in line with the cardinal points of the compass.

When she'd come to, Philip was apologizing for the sleeping

arrangements. "The college only booked one room, but I've been assured I can bring a guest." 'Business' indeed. She told him she'd think about it.

Shaking the suggestions hidden in both Philip's invitation and the description of the Callanish stones, Maggie took a drink of her coffee and returned her full attention to Sarah's broken picture frame.

She'd never really thought about it before, but the entire point of a picture frame was to make the viewer look at something else. Its job was to accentuate the photo without overpowering it. Frames for sale in a store usually had some sort of fake picture inside, and even the ones with words and decorations were still designed to highlight, not overpower, the image within.

So an empty picture frame fairly screamed in the silence of its omission.

She turned it over again and looked at the rectangle which had once housed an image important enough to Sarah MacKenzie to first display, then destroy. So many questions...

What picture was in here?

Why is the frame broken?

And, and she peered closer at the few glass shards embedded in the frame, *Is that blood?*

* * *

Just a trace. That's all she needed. Just some trace of the person.

Warwick sipped from her scalding coffee and allowed herself a smile as she opened her computer's browser. She enjoyed the challenge of it. Finding someone who didn't want to be found. It used to be more difficult, more challenging. Now, with credit checks for apartments and shopper's cards at grocery stores, it was harder to avoid being found. Most people didn't even think about it. It was the ones who did who were fun to hunt. Prey who knew the lion was watching.

With the grave-robbing case successfully delegated to Willis, Warwick had turned her attention fully to Benson's hotel murder. Ordinarily, she might not have been that interested in a homicide in another jurisdiction, but the connection to her local suicide had piqued Warwick's interest. Nevertheless, the leads were turning up dry. But that only meant other leads needed to be pursued. You might not be able to get blood from a stone, but you can get water from a cactus, if you know how to go about it. She knew one of those apparently dry leads was Devan Sinclair, the Aberdonian who had rented the room were the body was found.

His bookstore was closed and gone. His last known address was now someone else's flat. He had no known family alive. But Scotland wasn't that big of a country, and he couldn't use cash for everything.

Time to draw blood.

* * *

Maggie set the frame on her coffee table and knelt in front of it as if to pray. She had an idea of what she wanted to do, but wasn't sure of the details. A plan without a blueprint. A premise, but no script. A hope, but no words.

Well, some words. Probably. It was one of the spells she had, if not mastered, then at least used a few times, and therefore remembered. Mostly. She was pretty sure.

The divination spell. Extracting information from an object about a person who had been in contact with it. She'd used it a few times before and each time it had produced a vision for her to view. To date, she'd simply unleashed the spell and sat back to watch the phantasmic show that would coalesce in front of her face. This time, she wasn't entirely sure what to expect because she wasn't entirely sure if she could remember the spell correctly. She wondered what might happen if she got it a little bit wrong. Would it simply not work at all? Or would she get some other result, unsure how it might relate to the frame and Sarah?

Well, she thought, *only one way to find out.*

* * *

There was more than one way to find someone, Warwick knew. Or rather, there was more than one way for someone to give themselves away. Apartment application. Bank account. Debit card. Most people didn't even think about the cybertrail they left everywhere every day. You could tell the ones who did by how much less of a wake they generated. But refusing the supermarket discount card didn't do much if you still used your debit card to pay. Either way it was a blip on the screen.

Someone who had no blips at all—that's what stood out. Devan Sinclair was standing out. The last activity on that identity was the hotel room. She assumed he had come there on holiday.

Then she remembered: never assume.

She almost missed him.

* * *

Maggie closed her eyes and sighed. She really missed her Dark Book. But she supposed that's why she was pursuing the leads. Using what she could recall of the magic to track down the source of it. Or at least the user's manual.

She took a deep breath and tried to calm her thoughts. Then she opened her eyes again and spoke the spell—to the best of her recollection.

"<Release the secrets hidden inside this object.>"

Nothing happened at first, but that seemed to be the way sometimes with the magic, as if she were drawing water up from an ancient and weary well. After a moment, a small glow started right where she'd seen the dried blood on the broken glass. The glow swirled up and out from the frame in a billowing wisp, then coalesced into a translucent image before her amazed eyes.

They weren't amazed because the spell had worked. They were amazed because of what the spell showed her.

She recognized the scene. She just didn't know how it related to Sarah MacKenzie.

It was the murdered man, bloody and lifeless in the hotel bathtub.

* * *

Sinclair wasn't a ghost. He was a living breathing man. And he couldn't walk everywhere. If he'd merely been visiting Edinburgh, there was no reasonable way to guess where he might have been at any given moment of any particular day. But if he'd *moved* to Edinburgh, odds were good he'd used public transport. And there were cameras at every station.

His most recent driver's license photo was open on one of Warwick's two monitors. The link to Edinburgh's public safety cameras was on the other. It took a bit of an educated guess as to what kind of neighborhood a man like Sinclair might live in, but eventually her patience—and another refill of coffee—paid off.

She froze the frame. There he was. The morning commute into downtown. Looking up at the station clock—and the camera.

Edinburgh.

Devan Sinclair was in Edinburgh.

And now Warwick was going there too.

* * *

The hazy image had long since dissipated. Maggie had rocked back onto her backside and sat, silently, as she considered what was next. She knew what was next, but she felt an anxious emptiness in her stomach.

Edinburgh.

Iain was in Edinburgh.

And now Maggie was going there too.

21. Driven Crazy

A week later, Maggie had both begun the semester and made plans to leave the college. The good news was, Ellen was willing to drive. "A weekend in Edinburgh?" she'd said. "Count me in."

The bad news was, she had a really small car and had insisted on bringing a third person along.

The worse news was, the third person was a boy she'd just met and was sweet on.

The worst news was, it was Stuart Menzies.

"Maggie!" he fairly oozed when she stepped out of her flat toward Ellen's waiting car. "We meet again."

"You two know each other?" Ellen asked as she got out and popped open the compact's boot. Maggie shoved her backpack on top of the two bags already taking up most of the car's tiny storage space.

"We bumped into each other at the library," Stuart joked. "She was tripping all over herself when she met me."

Maggie groaned, but didn't say anything. She shoehorned herself into the alleged backseat. It was going to be a long drive.

* * *

The city of Arbroath lays approximately halfway between

Aberdeen and Edinburgh. It's a beautiful seaside village, looking out on the North Sea, and famous for the Declaration of Arbroath, a letter written in Arbroath Abbey in 1320, signed by three dozen Scottish nobles, and sent to Pope John XXII as an assertion of Scottish independence after the Pope had recognized the claim of the English king, Edward I, over Scotland and excommunicated the Scottish king, Robert the Bruce. In the Declaration, the Scots asserted they had the right to choose a king who would guarantee Scottish independence, and reserved to right to remove a king who failed to do so. It was one of the first expressions of popular sovereignty over divine right—another gift of the Scottish people to the world.

So Arbroath offered an ideal combination of Scottish beauty and Scottish history, surely a welcome destination for anyone even slightly interested in fair Alba. As they crossed into the picturesque and historical village, Maggie wished she could blow her brains out.

Stuart hadn't stopped talking since they'd left the parking spot in front of Maggie's flat. She wasn't sure he'd even paused to take a breath. To make it even worse, he hadn't addressed even one of his comments to his apparent girlfriend, Ellen Walker, preferring instead to speak exclusively with Maggie—ending statement after statement with, "Eh, Maggie?" The only times he wasn't talking directly to her were the rather common and astonishingly long monologues when he simply spewed forth information without any visible concern about who, or whether anyone, was listening.

It seemed that he had memorized that entire 'History of Science' book and was especially taken by the mortuary sciences. After discussing some of the less pleasant methods of disposing of bodies ("Zoroastrians believe fire and earth are primal forces which must not be contaminated by dead bodies, so they leave the bodies out to be picked clean by vultures, which is a bit of a problem now that most Zoroastrians live in big cities like Mumbai where there aren't many vultures any more. Pretty interesting, eh, Maggie?"), he moved on to a recitation of basic mummification practices.

"The ancient Egyptians used to pull the brain out through the nose with a hook," he announced. "That must've be pretty messy, eh, Maggie?"

Brain pulled out and mummified. Maggie wondered whether that's what had happened to Stuart. His skin did hold a rather unhealthy looking gray pallor. She decided not to reply. She'd actually stopped replying about an hour earlier, but he hadn't seemed to notice.

"What I find so interesting about that," he droned on, "is that we still do essentially the same thing. At autopsy, the coroner removes the brain, then sews it back up in the stomach cavity with the rest of the organs, all bagged together like a haggis. Sounds appetizing, eh, Maggie?"

Maggie realized he was using the split seconds after her name to breathe. That made her feel somehow responsible for her own torture.

"In a lot of ways," Stuart continued, "we don't really change. Science just gives us new ways of doing the same old things. Take alchemy for example. I'm studying chemistry, but I've also taken some courses on medieval history. Those alchemists were on the right track. They just never got it quite figured out, is all. They wanted to turn lead to gold, but it never worked. Maybe if they'd started with iron. And anyway, now we can make hydrogen from helium or, given enough energy, vice versa. I bet there are some lost secrets of those alchemists, things they knew were true but we can't see anymore because science is in the way, blinding us with the brilliance of its cold truth. Maybe some of those ancient secrets are just lying about under our noses, maybe even in one of the hundreds of dusty old books in the college's ancient book collections." This time, he turned and looked Maggie straight in the eye. "Eh, Maggie?"

Maggie met his gaze for several seconds, then closed her eyes and leaned her head against the car window. "I'm going to take a nap. You'll have to talk to Ellen for a while now."

And Stuart was silent for the remainder of the trip.

22. Maid to Order

They weren't staying at the Hotel Regency—not three students on a budget. And Maggie wasn't about to start flashing around her trust fund—not in front of Ellen, who didn't know about it, and certainly not in front of Stuart Menzies. The less he knew about her the better. Besides, the last thing she needed while she explored the Hotel Regency that afternoon was to run into either of them. So instead, they checked into the Hotel Rebus, a cheap but clean hotel about halfway between the main train station and the downtown core. It catered to students and budget-minded tourists, offering a small, clean room and little else. Maggie was relieved that she'd be sharing a room with Ellen while Stuart stayed across the hall. She didn't want them all to be in the same room, and she wanted even less for Ellen to share a room with him. They'd just met after all.

It took Maggie some convincing to extract herself from her companions for the afternoon, but not too much. Ellen was used to Maggie's sometimes mysterious ways, and she wanted some sight-seeing time alone with Stuart. He'd actually been the bigger issue, trying to insist that Maggie come along with them, but he was no match for two determined women. Maggie soon found her afternoon free and her plans in motion. They would all meet up at a pub near their hotel for dinner. Until then, Maggie would be at the Hotel Regency.

The trick wasn't getting there. Edinburgh had a very good public transportation system. The trick also wasn't getting inside. Anyone could walk into the lobby. No, the trick was getting into the room. The *same* room. She realized, as she approached the front doors of her destination, that she had no idea which room she had been in. She had no recollection of ever entering through the front door. But she realized the memory she did have might help her pinpoint its location anyway. She didn't remember going in, but she most definitely remembered going out. Out the window and onto the sidewalk by the loading dock. She stopped and considered for a moment, then turned to walk around back.

She arrived behind the hotel and scanned the area. Recalling the sting in her ankles, Maggie remembered that she'd dropped from the second floor. She looked up at the second floor windows, but they all looked the same. There was no sign with an arrow, saying, 'This One' or 'Dead Guy in Bathtub Suite.' So rather than looking up any more at the soft sandstone of the hotel, she looked down at the dull gray of the sidewalk. If she could remember where she landed, the room would be the second floor window directly above that.

Again, there was no magical 'Here' sign, but she recalled vividly the large woman who stormed at her from the loading dock. Keeping that mental image in mind, she shuffled slowly along the sidewalk until the angles and sightlines in her eyes corresponded with the memories in her mind. When she was pretty sure she'd found the right spot, she looked up and counted over. The window above her was fourth from the end.

Second floor. Facing the loading dock. Fourth from the end.

She put her fists on her hips and narrowed her eyes.

"Now... how do I get in?"

* * *

Emma Valentine held the print outs and doubled checked the alleles. It always took too long to get to all the testing they needed to do, but such was the life of a forensic scientist. Far more cases to solve than resources to solve them. So everything got in in line and waited its turn. But they'd finally gotten to that strange murder in the bathtub at the Hotel Regency and the wait had been worth it.

She turned and put her hands to her computer keyboard.

To: benson.lindsey@edinburgh.police.gov
From: valentine.emma@edinburgh.police.gov
Subject: DNA Result
I just completed the DNA work on the Hotel Regency case. One of the swabs from the scene contained a mixed sample. That is, there were two donors. That is, we have non-victim DNA at the scene, mixed with the victim's blood. Will draft formal report and forward ASAP.
-Emma

She clicked 'send' and smiled. "I wonder where that will lead."

* * *

Maggie's lip-twisted ruminations about how to slip into the Dead Guy Suite were interrupted—and, she realized after a moment, solved—by the loud clunk of the back door opening out onto the loading dock. A maid wheeled out a fabric-sided bin and left it there, dashing back inside before the heavy door slammed shut on her. Maggie hurried toward the loading dock. She couldn't see what was in the bin, but it didn't matter. If it wasn't laundry, she'd just steal a maid's uniform from inside.

* * *

The bin had not in fact been loaded with maid uniforms in just her size. It was flattened cardboard. But with her scheme fully formed and her resolve solidified, she walked back to the front of the hotel and casually strolled inside.

After a few excruciatingly long seconds clacking across the marble lobby where, thankfully, no one seemed to be paying any attention to her, she was able to slip into the cover of one of the long guest room hallways. The Dead Guy Suite was on two, but there was a maid cart dead ahead. It was cleaning time and the staff were doing their rounds. She had expected to find the laundry room first to grab a uniform but she knew an opportunity when she saw it. She scanned the cleaning cart as she approached. The maid was inside a room and Maggie's quarry was hanging by a strap from the cart. Without breaking stride, she yanked the passcard off the cleaning cart—the maid inside the room far too busy making the bed to notice—and disappeared into the next stairwell.

* * *

It took her longer to find the laundry than she'd expected. The hotel had a basement level, so that's where she'd started. It had looked promising, with concrete floors and undecorated hallways— just the sort of place one would expect to find a laundry room and supplies, especially maid uniforms. However, what few rooms there were housed things like boilers and plumbing and electrical. Necessary, Maggie supposed, but annoyingly unhelpful to her.

It took almost an hour before she found the extra maid uniforms in a supply closet on the sixth floor. As she slipped on the white coveralls and pink apron over her street clothes, she realized she probably could have been in and out of the Dead Guy Suite in the amount of time she'd taken searching for a maid outfit. She shrugged and tied the apron behind her back. Better to have a cover story if she were discovered. Not that she wanted that kind of complication—but she was learning to expect them.

She took the stairs back down to the second floor. There would be no elevator trips during this adventure. The hallway was quiet. Not 'too quiet,' but quiet. In fact, she might have welcomed some 'too quiet'—an eerie but empty hallway giving her the chance to slip into the room completely unnoticed. As it was, however, there were always a few guests walking from point A to point B. Luckily, her maid costume afforded her a measure of invisibility, as it signaled to the hotel patrons that it was socially acceptable to ignore her.

Nevertheless she kept her face turned down and away as she walked to the end of the hallway, then counted room doors on the way back.

One... Two... Three... Four. Dead Guy Suite.

She glanced around suspiciously, trying not to look it. There was one heavy-set man at the far end of the hallway near the vending machines. He was unlikely to notice her and even less likely to remember her. She pulled the passcard out of her apron pocket and slid it through the door's card reader. Two seconds and one flashing green indicator light later, she pushed open the door and slipped inside.

* * *

"I wonder if it's true," Emma Valentine remarked to her neighbor in the next cubicle, "that they always return to the scene of the crime."

"How's that, Emma?" replied Abby Jameson, the forensic scientist next to her. She had her face pressed against a microscope. "I'm kind of trying to concentrate here."

"I said, I wonder if it's true that they always return to the scene of the crime."

"Who?"

"The criminals."

Jameson lifted her face from the device. "Why would they do that?"

"I'm not sure," Valentine replied. "Maybe to see their handiwork."

"Oh, okay," Jameson said. Then after a moment. "So what?"

Valentine grinned. "Well, that's just it. If we can match the non-victim DNA, we could wait for the killer to return to the hotel room."

"You still going on about that hotel murder?" Jameson sighed. "Don't you have any other cases?"

Valentine tapped her lips. "I don't know, Abby. There's something about that one. Who removes a victim's spine?"

"Maybe it was my husband," Jameson joked. "He needs a backbone."

Valentine laughed and shook her head. "No, this was something sinister. I just hope we can match it before the killer's already been and gone."

* * *

Maggie scanned the hotel room. She wanted to do her thing and get out as fast as possible. The hour searching for the maid costume had given her extra time to consider the most efficient course of action. There had been blood on Sarah's picture frame, and there had been blood—lots of it—in the bathtub. The blood from the frame showed her the bathtub, so she wondered what the blood from the tub would show her.

'Nothing' was the apparent answer as she stepped into the bathroom.

It had been completely redone. Fresh paint and what seemed

to be a new shower. She pulled out her phone. The photo of the dead man was still there and pulling it up confirmed that the hotel management had—wisely, she supposed—completely replaced the shower/tub enclosure.

"Damn," she muttered. But she could hardly blame them. 'Mind the blood' was hardly a selling point.

She crossed her arms and frowned at the room. She'd come a long way and gone to a lot of trouble to just give up because of some entirely foreseeable redecorating. She raised a hand to her face and tapped pursed lips.

There were three choices. One, give up and leave now. That wasn't really an option. Not for her.

Two, figure out something else to inspect in the hotel room. Not bad, but still, an admission of defeat.

Or three, smash forward and figure out some way to make her original plan work.

Her frown curled into a smile. Option three it was. She had an idea.

She dug a fingernail into the caulk surrounding the shower enclosure. She scraped away until she got enough to grab, then she started peeling it off.

She doubted they bothered to paint under the new shower cover.

A few minutes later the caulk was curled up on the floor and the surprisingly thin plastic of the shower wall was pried away and propped open several inches by three wooden hangers from the closet. Maggie was peering into the gap, looking for bloodstains and wishing she'd remembered to bring her flashlight. Heck, she should have brought an entire toolkit, although she supposed that might have been suspicious: a maid with a tool box.

She peered into the gloomy gap, spying a myriad of stains

on the drywall. They had definitely not painted before the new, slightly larger shower had been installed. That left a thin strip of old white paint before the newer, yellow-beige color started. She decided that was her best bet and squinted low, guessing that any blood would likely be closer to the floor.

She wondered how the cops did it. How did they distinguish between blood stains and regular stains—mold, dirt, chocolate? She'd seen TV shows where they used some sort of test that made the blood glow in the dark or something. One more thing for her toolbox, she supposed. She located a small, dark stain near the floor. It was sort of a blotch with a half-hearted drip extending below it. It seemed like as good a candidate as any. She would have liked to have cut it out and taken it somewhere more conducive to the diving spell, but again no tool box, and anyway she didn't know what to use to cut drywall. She'd have to do the spell where she was, kneeling on the floor of a hotel bathroom in a maid costume. How dignified.

She reached into her pocket and pulled out the section of frame she had brought with her. She could hardly carry an entire picture frame in her pocket, and it was broken anyway, so she'd snapped off the side with the glass embedded into it. She laid it down next to the maybe-blood stain and prepared to cast the diving spell again.

She closed her eyes and took several deep breaths. She might not remember the exact words from the Dark Book, but she remembered the words she'd used on the frame back at her flat. She opened her eyes and said them again.

"<Release the secrets hidden inside this object.>"

Again, it took a moment, and again, she didn't know what to expect. She'd never cast the spell on two objects at once. But she cared about the connection between the stains more than anything else, and she couldn't think of a better way to find it out. As the glows began she wondered how they would interact. Would their rising mists combine to form a single image? Or would their images appear on top of each other, making it impossible to decipher either?

It turned out to be a little of both.

Two images arose, one from each location, next to each other but forming separately. Maggie had been expecting faces or people like she usually got—a scene unfolding, like a television show with the sound off. So it took her mind a few moments to realize what she was looking at. She had been most interested in the connection between the objects. The magic must have understood that and answered accordingly. She was looking at two glowing double-helixes—strands of DNA, rotating slowly before her eyes, their well-known twisted-ladder appearance easily recognizable to even the most science-averse person.

They spun slowly in front of her face, then began to float toward each other. As she watched, she noted something that was confirmed as the images reached each other and combined into a single, rotating strand of DNA.

They were identical.

There was only one conclusion: the blood from the frame was the dead man's. He had been in Sarah MacKenzie's apartment.

She just didn't know when. Or why. Or what it meant.

She also ran out of time to think about it. Someone was opening the hotel room door.

* * *

"Oh! I almost forgot the most important part," Valentine announced to no one in particular.

Jameson only offered a mumbled, "Hm?" as she continued her microscopic examination, but that was fine with Valentine. Her real audience was Det. Benson. She typed another email.

> *To: benson.lindsey@edinburgh.police.gov*
> *From: valentine.emma@edinburgh.police.gov*
> *Subject: One more thing*
> *The non-victim blood was XX. Whoever was in there, it was a*
> *woman.*
>
> *-E*

* * *

Maggie snatched up the frame piece and shoved it back into her pocket. There was no time to fix the shower. And no time, or place, to hide either. The door flew open with a slam and Maggie could do nothing but look through the bathroom door and feel her heart sink. It was the same large and unintelligible woman who'd spotted her by the loading dock weeks before.

"Yoo thar!" she bellowed. "Whut are yoo dooin' heer?"

Maggie closed her eyes. Her luck had finally run out.

"I tol' Mary tae cleen up theese rooms. Why isna she in heer a' doin' it?"

Or not. Maggie opened her eyes again, eager to take the opening the woman had just given her.

Then the woman noticed the carnage behind Maggie. "Good laird! Whut a' happened thar then?"

Maggie just shrugged. She knew better that to open her mouth and remind the woman of her accent.

"Did yoo find that then?" the woman asked.

Maggie nodded earnestly. Well, it wasn't really earnest, but she wanted it to look that way.

"Oh, good laird almighty!" The woman threw her hands up in despair. "Those gests will haff some esplainin' tae doo, I dare say." She pointed out into the hallway. "Goo an' get Mary. She needs tae see this afore those folks check oot."

Maggie nodded again and dashed into the hallway. She had no idea who Mary was, even less where she might be. But it didn't matter. She was getting the hell out of there.

23. Now I Really Need a Drink

Maggie sprinted down the first available stairwell. She pulled off the maid's uniform and stuffed it into a garbage can at the entrance to the first floor hallway. She slid the passcard under the door to the *men's* room off the lobby—the better to throw suspicion off of a female suspect. Then she darted outside into the safety of the warm Edinburgh afternoon.

She walked as fast as she could as far as she could until she felt her side splitting. When she finally slowed down, she figured she was at least a mile of winding streets away from the Hotel Regency and its Dead Man Suite.

By the time she'd made her way back to the right neighborhood and found the pub where she was meeting Ellen and Stuart, she was more than a little ready for a pint. What she wasn't ready for, but was nevertheless standing at the bar as she stepped up to order her drink, was Iain Grant.

He looked even more surprised than she was. Of course, she at least knew they were both in the same city. He actually spilled his drink on himself when he saw her.

"M-Maggie?" he managed to stammer. "What are you doing here?"

She wasn't ready for this. Sure, she knew they were in the

same city. Sure, she figured she might run into him somewhere. But she expected that to be someplace like downtown, where everybody went sometimes. What the hell was he doing in a pub near some dumpy hotel Ellen had picked because it was cheap? And why did he have to be so goddamn handsome? No, she was definitely not ready for this. *Deflectors to full force.*

"I could ask you the same thing," she replied.

Hey, it worked last time.

"What am *I* doing here?" he repeated, dumbfounded. "I live here."

She crossed her arms. "So I hear."

Iain crossed his too and glanced around. "You're not here to see me, are you?" he realized. "This is one of your little junkets."

"Junket?" Maggie sneered. "Nobody really says 'junket.' And anyway, it's none of your business. So don't judge me. You gave up your right to judge me when you walked away."

"You never gave me a chance to judge you," Iain countered.

"And now I know why," Maggie rejoined. "You would have walked away."

"I walked away because you lied to me," Iain defended, "not because of what I saw."

Maggie shook her head. "Don't pretend you didn't know I was keeping secrets. You knew. You loved it. You were all, 'Ye're a mysterious lass, ye are, Maggie Deveroo,' and 'Och, me wee lassie's got her secrets, she doo.'"

Iain crossed his arms and tried to look offended. But the faintest of smiles alighted in the corner of his mouth. "That's not what I sound like."

"That is exactly what you sound like," Maggie replied. Her own smile crept into the corner of her own mouth, much to her irritation. "And anyway, that's not the point. You knew. You didn't know it all, but you knew. I trusted you and you walked away."

Ian's eyebrows shot up. The smile disappeared. "Trusted me? That's exactly what you didn't do. You didn't trust me. You don't trust me."

"I did," Maggie protested. Then she set her jaw and looked down. "And damn it, even if you don't deserve it, I still do."

Iain uncrossed his arms. "You do?"

Maggie frowned and lowered her own arms. She looked up at him "Yes."

He nodded for several moments. He looked down at his drinks for several seconds more, obviously in thought. Then he took a deep breath and looked up again. "Prove it."

"What?" Maggie was stunned by the sudden demand.

"Prove it," Iain repeated. "Tell me exactly what you're doing here in Edinburgh. You're not sight-seeing, I know that. Tell me the truth."

Maggie's heart exploded with adrenaline. Conflicting emotions cascaded over her. She'd never willfully shared the magic with anyone. It was ingrained to keep it secret. Besides, where did she start? The Lost Weeks? The murdered man in the bathtub? Could she trust him that far? Or would he call the police? Magic was one thing, murder was another. Besides, you don't test trust. You accept it. You earn it. Demanding proof of it unearned it. Her anger in being challenged, coupled with her fear of being turned in, overcame her longing to rest her cheek on his chest again.

"I'm sight-seeing," she asserted. "With Ellen. And her new boyfriend. That's all."

They both knew she was lying.

It felt like someone had just died.

She fought off the regret clawing at her heart. She made an ill-advised decision to go on the offensive. She glanced around. "So is that tramp here with you?"

Iain nearly spilled his drink again. "Heather's not a tramp," he shot back.

"Heather?" Maggie repeated the name and rolled her eyes. "Oh, well, what a bonnie Scottish name that it. Och and haggis and all that."

Iain set his chiseled jaw. "Don't be a—" But he stopped himself.

"Oh please." Maggie swirled her hand at him. "Finish your thought. Don't be a what?"

Iain narrowed his eyes. "The word I was going to use started with B," he admitted. "Then I thought of changing it to 'witch,' but I thought you might think it was a compliment."

Maggie shook her head and swallowed the lump in her throat. It wasn't supposed to be like this.

And it certainly wasn't supposed to be like what happened next. The tramp arrived. Heather. Bonnie wee Heather.

She stepped up and stood way too close to Iain. She looked Maggie up and down, not even trying to hide her disdain. "Who's this?" she sneered.

"Maggie," Iain answered woodenly. He didn't look away from Maggie. But he didn't move away from Heather either.

"Oh," said Heather. That was it. No, 'Nice to meet you.' No 'I've heard a lot about you.' Which told Maggie that Heather had heard a lot about her and it was not nice to meet her.

Heather slipped her arm through Iain's. He stiffened a bit, but didn't resist. "So what brings you to Edinburgh, Maggie?" she asked. "Are you really that desperate?"

Maggie immediately felt better about not liking Heather. It was one thing to be a rival. It was another to be a 'witch.'

"Hardly," Maggie replied. "I'm here for something else."

"Oh really?" Heather took a sip from her beer. "What's that?"

"I'd rather not say," Maggie demurred.

"Typical," Iain grunted and glanced away.

Maggie had gone through a lot of emotions that afternoon. Worry about her plan. Satisfaction at it working. Panic at being discovered. Relief at escaping. Surprise at encountering Iain. Sadness at their conversation. Jealousy at seeing Heather. She'd just about had it.

"Excuse me?" she demanded of the tall Scotsman.

He hesitated, clearly recognizing the edge to her tone, and a bit surprised at being called out on his comment. But the beer in his hand and the blonde on his arm seemed to fortify his courage. "I said it was typical. You're off to some distant city, on some secret mission, and when the opportunity presents itself to be honest about what you're doing, you clam up. Do you even know how to be honest?"

Maggie narrowed her eyes and crossed her arms. "I'd like to have someone to talk to, but he'd have to be somebody pretty special. Strong. Understanding. Trustworthy."

Iain's own eyes narrowed. "It's hard to trust when the trust's been broken."

"It goes both ways," Maggie shot back. "A true friend is ready to trust when the time is right."

Heather had faded into irrelevance as Maggie and Iain locked eyes.

"Just a friend, eh?" Iain scoffed. "Is that all I was? Well, then go tell a friend. Go tell Ellen."

"Tell me what?" Ellen walked up just then, Stuart peering wraithlike over her shoulder. She ignored Heather. "Hello, Iain."

He nodded stiffly to her. Heather tightened her grip. She

was suddenly outnumbered.

"Tell me what?" Ellen repeated.

"Secrets," Iain answered glumly.

Ellen flashed a saccharine smile, her large teeth beaming, and turned to her American friend. "Oh, no. Don't tell me, Mags. Tell someone you can really trust. Tell Philip."

"Philip?" Iain asked far too quickly, the shock—and pain—obvious in his voice.

Maggie wasn't sure what to say. Ellen was.

"Oh, aye." She looked back to Iain and laid it on thick. "A handsome young professor. He's from Vancouver, Canada, right by Maggie's own hometown. He's just arrived in Aberdeen and teaches some of the very subjects Maggie here is studying. And..." She winked at Maggie. "I think he's taken a rather obvious shine to our Maggie here."

Maggie felt herself blush, but she didn't stop Ellen.

Ellen tipped her head slightly and addressed the woman attached to Iain's arm. "I think it's important to be with someone who really understands you. Don't you agree?"

Heather provided a cold smile and hugged Iain's arm. "Oh, yes. I agree completely."

Maggie ignored Heather. And Ellen. And especially Stuart. She stared up at Iain. He was staring right back at her.

Finally she looked down. "Goodbye. Iain."

Iain nodded. "Goodbye, Maggie."

And they went their separate ways.

24. Everything in Its Place

Maggie drank way too much. The shared room with Ellen turned out to be doubly smart. She doubted she'd ever had made it back without her. She recalled being dumped into the bed. If she'd cared about whether Ellen stayed, such concern evaporated when the nightmare started.

This time she was already in the grave. All the way at the bottom. There was no coffin, just cool, damp earth. She was looking up from the bottom, her back cold and wet, her head heavy and dirty. Clouds passed in front of the half moon that illuminated her grave.

The walls were too high to climb. She almost didn't even bother trying. It would be easier to just give up and accept her fate. She felt exhausted, her shoulders achy and her limbs leaden. But she forced herself to her feet and reached for the grassy top, trying to wedge her shoes into the sides of the earthen vault.

It was no use. The surface was just out of her reach and her shoes couldn't find any footholds. She scrambled and scrambled, but got nowhere. Her front was filthy, smeared and caked with mud. She was out of breath. Her arms ached. Her knees were scraped. She would try one more time, then resign herself to her doom.

She extended her hands as far up as she could.

She jumped as high as she could.

She didn't quite reach the top.

But she didn't fall back to the bottom either.

A hand reached over and grabbed her wrist. A man's hand. A strong hand.

She grabbed her savior's arm and felt her heart lighten as she was pulled from the pit. She landed on the grass and looked up at the man who'd saved her life. They were still holding hands.

It was Iain.

She didn't know what to say.

He didn't say anything.

Instead he let go of her wrist and knelt down next to her, smiling.

She propped herself into a half-sitting position and smiled back—then shoved him into the grave with her feet. He fell to the bottom with a damp thud. She looked over the edge to see him lying in a twisted heap.

He was starting to move, so she pulled the shovel out of the pile of dirt next to her and began filling the grave.

25. Big Dig

Edinburgh Castle has stood for centuries atop its grand hill, surveying the city below, the harbor, and the icy waters of the North Sea beyond. Its rambling parapets and granite face paid tribute to its history as both a political and military institution. From long before the time of the Stuart kings to the modern day, the castle towered over the daily lives of the Scottish capitals' inhabitants, from their births at home and hospital, to their young days in the schools, to their weddings in the churches, to their first jobs at the factories, and finally to the unavoidable end of all lives and their final internment in one of the city's many cemeteries.

In one such cemetery, well-known for many reasons, the castle would have been visible from the grounds, but for the dense trees and the dark night. Instead, the pale sliver of moonlight illuminated only the bleached headstones and the rusted blade of a shovel as it cleaved the ground and turned, tearing the roots of the living grass from the death-concealing dirt beneath.

Shhk. Shhk. Shhk.

Dig. Turn. Toss. Dig. Turn. Toss. Dig. Turn. Toss.

There was time. No time to waste. But still time to use.

Shhk. Shhk. Shhk,

26. Sinclair

There came a knock at his door. Loud. Staccato. Professional.

Devan Sinclair pushed away from his breakfast table. His toast and coffee would have to wait. He'd learned it wasn't the late night knocks that were to be feared; it was the early morning ones. And if not, feared, at least respected. Early risers rarely took no for an answer.

He peered out the peephole to confirm his suspicion, then opened his door.

"Good morning, officers."

"Good morning, Mr. Sinclair," said the shorter of the two women standing in his hallway—the blonde one, with the funereal expression. Each wore a non-descript suit and displayed a badge on her belt.

Sinclair assumed he was supposed to be impressed by their knowing his name. He wasn't particularly. He stepped back and invited them inside.

For his part, he was dressed in gray slacks with a matching gray vest and a crisp white shirt. His dark blond hair was combed straight back and his face was freshly shaved, save the well-groomed goatee, making the scar down his left cheek unmistakable.

He was an early riser as well.

"I'm inspector Lindsey Benson of the Edinburgh Police," the taller officer identified herself as she put away her badge and entered the flat. "This is Sergeant Elizabeth Warwick of the Aberdeen Police. Do you have time for a few questions?"

"Of course." Sinclair closed the door behind them and returned to his seat at his breakfast table. He gestured for them to join him. "I'm always happy to help the authorities."

Warwick and Benson sat down at Sinclair's small kitchen table. There were chairs for four, but breakfast was for one. Just as well. They'd eaten on the way over.

Benson started the questioning. It was her city. "Are you familiar with the Hotel Regency downtown?"

Sinclair nodded as he swallowed a bite of food. He dabbed his mouth with his napkin. "I would prefer it," he said, "if you'd just come out with it. Please don't try to trick me into admitting something which will be easily explained away as a misunderstanding caused by your being overly coy. Simply tell me why you're here and what you want to know."

The officers hesitated. Each looked at the other for some indication of how to respond. Warwick gave it first. She sighed.

"Fine," Warwick said. "There was a murder several weeks at the Hotel Regency here in Edinburgh. It was fairly grisly. The victim was found in the bathtub with blood everywhere and a flat stone across his eyes."

Sinclair kept his face expressionless. "Yes? And?"

"And your name was on the registry," Benson jumped in. "In fact, that was the last time you came up in any electronic transactions anywhere. You just fell off the face of the Earth after that."

Sinclair looked around his small, but comfortable flat. "I've fallen nowhere, I assure you. I've been here the entire time."

Benson leaned onto the table. "Why did you rent that room? And how did a dead man end up in the bathtub?"

Sinclair resisted leaning away from the inspector. Instead, he held his ground and replied, "I have no idea how a dead man ended up in the bathtub. And I did not rent that room."

"It's your name on the registry," Benson repeated. "Your credit card number was used."

"My credit card number was stolen," Sinclair replied, "and used rather irresponsibly until I closed the account. Whoever stole it rented that room, purchased some very expensive electronics, opened several adult internet accounts, and even donated to the Tories. None of which I approved."

Benson narrowed her eyes at him. "Did you report the theft?"

"No," was the simple answer.

"Why not?" Benson pressed.

"Would you have caught them?" Sinclair challenged.

Benson hesitated. "Maybe."

Sinclair shook his head. "Unlikely at best. Identity theft may be trendy, but it's still just theft. Your department has too many other, more serious crimes to pursue, and already not enough officers to do it."

Benson could hardly argue with that.

"Why Edinburgh?" Warwick interjected.

Sinclair understood the question. "I needed a change. A fresh start."

"Why was that?"

Sinclair met Warwick's gaze directly. "I don't think I need to explain that to you, do I, Sergeant?"

Benson looked puzzled. Warwick didn't. Just the opposite,

actually.

"Is that all?" Sinclair asked, standing up. "I need to get about my day."

"Not quite," Benson answered. She removed the clan crest pendant from her pocket. "Do you recognize this?"

Sinclair looked at the baggie for several seconds. "I've seen them before," he answered, "but I don't know whose that is."

Benson smiled and returned the evidence to her pocket. "All right then. Thank you, Mr. Sinclair."

Warwick thanked him as well and they let themselves out as Sinclair cleared his dishes. Once in the hallway, Benson turned to Warwick. "Well, that last bit was interesting anyway."

Warwick agreed, but likely for different reasons. "How so?"

Benson pulled out the pendant again. "He didn't ask us where we found it. And he assumed we cared whose it is."

27. The Best Laid Plans

The rest of Maggie's night was a painful drunken blur, but when she woke, the memory of burying Iain alive was as fresh as if it were happening right then.

Ignoring, as best she could, the brick lodged behind her eyes, she rose, showered, and went down to the hotel lobby for breakfast. She also decided to ignore that Ellen wasn't in their room when she woke up, preferring to believe she had simply gotten up first and would be waiting downstairs.

In addition to a clean, cheap room, Hotel Rebus also offered a continental so-called breakfast. One of the advantages of having eschewed The Continent for The Isles was regularly enjoying a breakfast that consisted of more than ten versions of bread. Then again, she thought, as she placed a hard roll and an even harder roll on her plate, any attempt at eggs or sausage right then would likely have resulted in some rather violent vomiting. Maybe the Continentals were just hung-over more often than the Brits.

Maggie found a small table in the back corner of the breakfast room. There were a few others also breaking their fasts just then. One was reading the paper, two were talking to each other, another was intently buttering his roll, and all of them were, like her, trying to ignore the large-screen TV blasting at them from its spot covering most of the main wall.

Maggie's eyes would not have taken kindly to being asked to focus on newsprint just then, so she decided not to seek out a discarded section of newspaper. She didn't have anyone to talk to. And she didn't want any butter on either of her rolls. So she sighed and surrendered to Mr. Orwell's ubiquitous screen.

There were two hosts on the morning program: one man and one woman. Both were plasticly pretty, with broad smiles as fake as the seascape projected behind them. The bubbly blonde woman was giggling as she finished the latest story. "...and I bet that cute little kitty-cat will stay away from that sandwich-slicer from now on."

She turned to her co-host and cued the next story. "Liam?"

"Thanks, Kelsey." He grinned at her, then turned back to the camera. Maggie took a bite from the harder roll and chewed with begrudging interest.

"Grave robbers struck the Greyfriars Kirkyard last night," Liam reported with a suddenly somber expression, "digging up the grave of a woman named Rebecca NicInnes Adams. Although police haven't released details as to what might have been taken, the crime matches similar recent grave robberies from as far away as Aberdeen."

Maggie dropped her roll. It clanked off the plate and onto the floor, but she paid it no attention. She was riveted to the TV. So of course, that's exactly when Ellen and Stuart walked in.

"Maggie!" Ellen called out over the television and hurried to her table. "There you are. None too worse for wear, I see. Did you sleep all right, then?"

Maggie craned her neck to try to see around Ellen, but it was too late. Mr. and Mrs. MacSmiley had moved on to a story about remote-controlled boats in some city fountain somewhere. She sighed and returned her gaze to her friend.

"I slept okay," she said. Then she rubbed the back of her neck and added, "Strange dreams, though."

"Well, too much Scottish beer will do that, eh?" Ellen grinned. Then she excused herself to fetch something to eat. Stuart followed her and in a few minutes they returned to Maggie' table, eating breakfast and ready to plan their day, unaware that Maggie's plans—whatever they might have been—had changed.

"So what shall we do today?" Ellen asked.

Maggie knew exactly what she was doing that day. The question was how to ditch Ellen and Stuart so she could do it.

"I was thinking we could go to the National Museum," Stuart suggested. "They're having an exhibit on the greatest advances of science."

No chance in Hell, Maggie thought. "Maybe," she said. "Could I see your tour book, Ellen?"

Ellen had bought the latest guide to the Scottish capital when Maggie had asked for the ride. She'd been to Edinburgh plenty of times before, Ellen had explained, but always liked going with someone else because it gave her a chance to play tourist in her own country. Maggie flipped through the pages, looking for a map of the city, and specifically one with Greyfriars Kirkyard. When she found it, the write-up on the opposite page confirmed she'd be going there that day.

Commissioned in 1561 by Mary Queen of Scots because the cemetery at St. Giles Cathedral (see page 37) was full, Greyfriars Kirk Cemetery is reported to be one of the most haunted spots in all of Scotland. The most famous ghost is that of 'Bluidy' George MacKenzie, which is reported to attack tourists, leaving bite and scratch marks. Sir George MacKenzie was the Lord Advocate of

Scotland from 1677-1688 and was an accomplished lawyer and novelist. One of his more notable cases came defending a woman accused of witchcraft in the Midlothian witchcraft trials of 1661, although, as he explained at the time, not because there were no such things as witches, but rather that they were rarer than people thought.

The south end of the graveyard contains many enclosed vaults and two 'mort-safes'—low, iron-work cages covering temporary graves which could be rented out until the bodies had decomposed enough to no longer be of interest to the grave-robbing "resurrection men" who provided Edinburgh Medical College with fresh bodies before the 1832 Anatomy Act began allowing, and regulating, the use of corpses for medical purposes.

Maggie looked up from the book. MacKenzie? Grave robbers? Witches?! Oh yes, she was going to Greyfriars Kirkyard. She just needed to ditch Ellen and Stuart.

She'd gotten pretty good at ditching people and actually had begun to categorize the different types of ditches by timing and type. The previous day had been a ditch-in-advance, a planned separation allowing her to pursue what she needed to pursue. That likely wouldn't work again. Ellen seemed intent on spending time with her that day, which meant Stuart would be around too. So Maggie needed to use a ditch-of-opportunity, disappearing either with some pre-planned excuse or when her companions were distracted, then explaining it later.

She looked at the map. For better and worse, Greyfriars Kirkyard was basically across the street from the National Museum. She sighed.

"Stuart," she forced herself to say, "I think you're right. Let's go to the National Museum's exhibit of that science junk or whatever."

Stuart was so surprised—either by Maggie agreeing, or by her being nice about it, or, most likely, the combination of those two things—that his bite of roll actually fell out of his mouth. Not very appealing. Maggie was officially done with breakfast.

"Uh, wow," Stuart stammered. "That's great. Brilliant. Thank you."

He looked down at his soggy, half-eaten roll bite. "Maybe I'd better get a new roll," he said, and hurried away before Maggie could change her mind.

Once he was out of earshot, Ellen reached over and grabbed Maggie's hand. "Thanks, Mags. I know you don't really want to go to the museum, but Stuart's right keen on all that science stuff."

"No problem," Maggie answered with a smile. "I'm sure I'll dig up something to interest me too."

28. Science through the Ages

The National Museum of Scotland was everything one would expect. Only blocks from Edinburgh Castle, it was absolutely enormous, resulting from the merger of three previous museums: the National Museum of Antiquities of Scotland, the Royal Scottish Museum, and the Museum of Scotland. Boasting sixteen exhibit halls behind its Victorian Romanesque facade, it was the depository to some of Scotland's most venerable national treasures. With over 8,000 objects on display, it would take a full day just to see a fraction of the art collection, let alone its exhibits on natural history, archaeology, and technology. It was a pinnacle of Scottish history and achievement.

Maggie couldn't wait to get out of there.

The 'Science through the Ages' exhibit was housed in one of the rotating exhibits halls at the far end of the museum. That is, it was about as far away from Greyfriars as possible. Just walking from the hall to the front door of the museum was going to take her five full minutes. She'd just have to hope the exhibit was enthralling enough to keep Stuart and Ellen from really noticing she was gone. In addition to the ten minutes through the museums corridors—five on the way there, five on the way back—she figured another fifteen to find the grave and ten to fifteen to poke around and discover whatever it was she was hoping to find. So, all in all, she'd be gone about forty-five minutes. They'd probably notice her disappearance by then, but likely wouldn't have done much about it yet. The museum was big enough she could suddenly reappear and credibly claim to have gotten lost looking for the restroom.

The exhibit itself was divided into several sub-exhibits, starting with 'Pre-History,' then clumping groups of years together. The farther back in time one went, the more years were combined into a group. For example, '500 B.C.E.-1500 A.D.' took up one room, while the years '1950-present' were afforded the same amount of space. Maggie supposed science was an accelerating field, so that as the ball really got going, the pace of invention increased as well. Still, she guessed there was a certain bias against the knowledge of the ancients, born of ignorance. We didn't know what we didn't know.

One display in the 'Pre-History' section illustrated her point. It was a model of Stonehenge. Feeling a private connection to the mysterious standing stones of Salisbury Plain, Maggie stepped over to the display as Ellen and Stuart dissipated into the rest of the exhibit.

No one knows for sure why the giant formation at Stonehenge was built. It clearly held an astronomical use, as evinced by the manner in which its layout aligns with the rising sun on the equinox and solstices. But there are many who believe it must have served some greater purpose to have motivated those who erected it to move monumental stones over hundreds of miles. Most such theories claim a religious or political significance. Others point to its location along what have been termed the 'ley' lines of the planet. One recent theory even suggested the stones at Stonehenge were some sort of recording device, preserving in

psychic vibration the knowledge of the ancients. But the truth
about Stonehenge is that no one really knows why it was built.

Maggie finished reading, then looked up and around. Ellen and Stuart were nowhere to be seen. She considered leaving just then, but the exhibit was commanding her interest despite herself. She began to wonder what scientific advances might have been achieved back at the time of Brìghde Innes. Walking though the sub-exhibits, she quickly found the one marked 'A.D. 1500-1700.'

Thankfully the stagers of the exhibit seemed to appreciate that not everyone might share an enthusiasm for scientific minutiae commensurate with that of Stuart Menzies'. Although there were certainly displays about the advancement of the most esoteric and specialized technologies, the more well-known advancements were given greater treatment, not unlike the Stonehenge model near the entrance, set out in larger, more visibly-interesting displays. The first of these in the '1500-1700' section was a miniature solar system at the very center of the room. There were only six planets, but it didn't take long for Maggie to realize the significance wasn't the number of planets, but rather, their position relative to the sun and Earth. She was used to seeing the sun at the center of solar system models; the people of the 1500s, not so much. The plaque on the side of the display explained it more fully.

In ancient times and throughout the Middle Ages, it was accepted as self-evident and theologically significant that the Earth was the center of the universe, and specifically that the planets and the sun orbited the Earth just as did the moon. In 1543, shortly before his death, Nicolaus Copernicus (1473-1543) published De revolutionibus orbium coelestium *(On the Revolutions of the Heavenly Spheres), which set forth his theory of a heliocentric solar system. Although his sun-centered model was simpler than Ptolemy's Earth-centered model, and accorded better with empirical astronomical observations, it was quite controversial because it challenged the prevailing religious view that the Earth was the center of all creation.*

Copernicus' model was vindicated nearly a hundred years later by two related events. In 1631, French astronomer Pierre Gassendi (1592-1655) documented the transit of both Mercury and Venus across the sun, confirming that these planets lay between the sun and Earth. Then, in 1632, Italian astronomer Galileo Galilei (1564-1642) published his Dialogo sopra i due massimi sistemi del mondo *(Dialogue Concerning the Two Chief World Systems), wherein he established the superiority of the Copernican model. For this, as well as for the disrespectful tone of the book toward Pope Urban VIII (1568-1644), Galileo was tried and convicted of heresy, forced to recant his championing of the heliocentric model, and spent the remainder of his life under house arrest.*

Nevertheless, the model of the universe explained by Copernicus and championed by Galileo prevailed, becoming a prime example of the power of science to reveal the truth even when such truth runs counter to prevailing beliefs. This development is often cited as the beginning of a new scientific age of reason where science first established its superiority over superstition.

Maggie looked back to the model with its large orange sun in the center. Sometimes, the most obvious truths can be obscured by our everyday observations. She looked around the room for any similar major displays. The only other was a portrait on the opposite wall of a man wearing what was, by modern standards anyway, an absolutely ridiculous wig. The painting looked familiar somehow. If nothing else, its style reminded her of the portrait of Brìghde in the art book. It hung centered on the wall, a light suspended above it, and obviously in a place of honor. She stepped over and read the plaque next to it.

Sir Isaac Newton (1642-1727). Physicist and mathematician.

Perhaps no one has had as great an impact on the advancement of science as Sir Isaac Newton. In addition to his invention of infinitesimal calculus (also developed independently by German mathematician Gottfried Wilhelm Leibniz (1646-1716)), Newton is best known for his monumental work, Philosophiæ Naturalis Principia Mathematica *(Mathematical Principles of Natural Philosophy). In it, Newton laid out his laws of motion, now commonly referred to as the Newtonian Laws, which were significant not only because they explained perfectly the motion of both small objects (an apple falling from a tree) and large objects (the moon orbiting the sun), but also because they were true independent of any higher meaning or intent. They simply were true and always had been and always would be, which meant they could be relied upon for future scientific and industrial development. When Newton published his* Principia *in 1687, he laid the groundwork for our modern science-based world.*

Next to the portrait, on a pedestal, was a reproduction of Newton's great work, laid open to some undoubtedly significant page. Underneath it, a plaque read, 'The Book that Unlocked the Natural World.'

Hm, Maggie thought noncommittally. There were still a few secrets left.

She continued to wander through the exhibit, from era to

era, until she found herself in the final room, the one with the most recent scientific advancements. She was so caught up in trying to understand the displays about subatomic hocus-pocus and quantum voodoo that she wasn't watching where she was going and once again tripped over Stuart Menzies, who was crouched down to get a better view at some display Maggie didn't even want to try to understand.

"Oh, Maggie!" he beamed, despite the general rudeness of being stepped on. "We have to stop running into each other like this."

Maggie managed a weak nod at the joke. She wished she'd stayed back in the steam power displays.

"Look at this one," Stuart said excitedly, pointing at a display of a stuffed sheep. "This is Dolly."

"Dolly," Maggie repeated, as if she were supposed to know. 'Dolly the Sheep' did sound familiar. Like a children's story.

"The first mammal to be cloned from an adult somatic cell, using the process of nuclear transfer," Stuart explained. Well, sort of explained. Maggie understood 'first,' 'mammal,' and 'cloned.' That was probably enough.

"Oh," Maggie replied. She'd heard of that.

"Oh?" Stuart questioned her reaction. "Just 'oh'? No, it's much more than 'oh.' It was the culmination of the greatest scientific riddle ever: the creation of life itself. Life is biology and biology is just chemistry, but still, there's something special, intangible, almost magical about life. Humankind has always longed to create life, to resurrect the dead, the beat back the natural and inescapable cycle of life and death, whether it was Mary Shelly or the Scottish scientists who cloned Dolly. The dream has always been the same, to unlock the secret of life. And this is exactly when we did it."

Maggie looked at the plaque. She was just a little girl when it had happened. And she didn't usually like thinking about that time in her life. It was time to ditch.

"I have to pee," she announced, and walked briskly away.

Stuart Menzies watched after her and smiled.

29. Greyfriars Kirkyard

The street between the museum and the graveyard—Candlemakers Row—was a bit busier than Maggie would have liked. It wasn't a major thoroughfare, but the traffic was relentless that time of day. She had to check her impulse to dash across the street, and forced herself to wait for the cars to clear. No use in becoming a ghost herself.

A few long minutes later, she'd made it safely across the street and looked up at the main gate to the kirkyard. It was wrought iron with the word 'GREYFRIARS' along the top. Just inside there was a statue of a dog. She walked over and read the inscription. It was devoted to 'Greyfriars Bobby,' a terrier who slept atop his policeman master's grave for over a decade after his death.

Now that was loyalty, Maggie thought. *Certain Scottish men named Iain could learn a thing or two from that dog.*

Then she shook her head. No, no thinking about Iain. Iain was the past. She had to think about the future. Getting her Book back and starting over. Moving forward.

What better place to start over than a graveyard? She shook her head again at the irony. At least she wasn't whistling.

Looking around, Maggie realized the grounds were more expansive than they'd seemed on the tour book map. Fifteen minutes might not be enough time to locate the defiled grave of her ancestor. Tourists milled about casually. There was nothing indicating the recent commission of a crime. She pursed her lips and tapped her foot, trying to decide which of four paths to take. Then she thought better of guessing and scanned the entry for a map. She found it off to the side, near the front gate.

The oldest graves were to her right. That was where she would find Rebecca's grave—or what was left of it. MacKenzie's mausoleum and the South Yard with its mort-safes were to her left. Decisions, decisions. But the paths encircled the kirkyard and connected at the back. She could go to her right and if she located the open grave quickly enough, she'd have enough time to circle back by MacKenzie and the anti-grave robber contraptions on her way out.

The grass was a deep, lush green, broken artistically by scores of gray stone monuments and headstones. Low-hanging branches shaded her way and a beautiful sandstone church—'kirk,' she reminded herself—rested sphinx-like at the center of the grounds. It was around this house of worship that the circuitous route would take her.

She walked quickly, the time limits on her ditch-of-opportunity weighing on her mind and speeding her feet. She wasn't entirely sure how much time she'd need at the gravesite. At least enough to read the headstone, peer into the grave, and identify some useful clue she could slip into pocket for later examination. Three to five minutes, she supposed. She took a bend in the sidewalk, ducked under a branch, and realized she'd be getting that three to five minutes back.

Ahead and to the right was very obviously the grave she was looking for. It was obvious for three reasons: one, the mound of black earth piled up next to it; two, the blue and white police tape wrapped around a nearby tree and two headstones cordoning off the grave from the rest of the kirkyard; and three—much to Maggie's chagrin—the uniformed policeman standing guard.

"Damn," she hissed. She should have realized it might be guarded. She hadn't expected the police to need to guard a grave, but she supposed the crime was still pretty fresh, having just been discovered that morning. She frowned, but shrugged. There was nothing to be done just then. Maybe Stuart would want to go back to the museum again tomorrow.

She put her hands in her pockets and set out to complete her circuit. The South Yard was intriguing, jutting out from the rest of the cemetery like a long, rectangular peninsula, a gangplank of sorts, filled with fortifications against the grave robbers from the dawn of the Age of Science. *Savages.* She wondered if Stuart's exhibit included a display on the resurrectionists. She shrugged again. Probably. *Damn scientists.*

The mort-safes were especially intriguing. They were iron cages, only a foot or two high, each covering two temporary grave holes. The purpose was to allow the bodies to decompose enough to be of no use to the doctors. To that end, Maggie realized why the South Yard might have been set off so distinctly from the rest of the serene cemetery. It must have smelled terrible.

She surveyed the area one more time, wishing something similar to a mort-safe had encased her ancestor, then headed for the exit. Bluidy MacKenzie's mausoleum would be on her way out.

If she hadn't known where it was by the map in her head, the gaggle of tourists grouped in front of the circular, domed mausoleum would have tipped her off. As she approached, her deduction was confirmed by the tour guide who was standing in front of the mausoleum and regaling the crowd with a bit about Sir George's ghost. Having been denied the opportunity to poke around Rebecca's grave, Maggie supposed she had time to listen to at least some of the tour guide's practiced spiel.

"This is the tomb of Sir George MacKenzie," the tour guide said. She was a young woman with red hair pulled back into a fuzzy ponytail and sporting a utilitarian backpack over her shoulders. "Also known as 'Bluidy MacKenzie,' he was the Lord Advocate of Scotland, and during the War of the Three Kingdoms, he sided with the Crown against the so-called 'Covenanters,' a group of devout Presbyterians who at one time were the *de facto* government of Scotland. A walled-off section of the cemetery was converted to an outdoor prison for the Covenanters, and MacKenzie oversaw the running of the prison. He was responsible for the torture and execution of its prisoners. The fact that he was interred so close to those whom he tormented may explain the high level of paranormal activity associated with the MacKenzie Poltergeist. Visitors here have reported strange sounds and smells, feeling general unease and unexplained drops in temperature, and even being attacked—receiving scratches and bite marks. In fact, the attacks grew to such a frenzied level that the Covenanters Prison is now locked off to the general public and accessible only on our nightly City of the Dead tours."

"Oh! Is there a tour tonight?" asked one of the tourists.

"Aye," the tour guide replied with a grin. "Every night after the sun sets."

Maggie grinned too. She knew what she was doing that night.

* * *

Maggie was almost as surprised by how easily Ellen and Stuart accepted her lost bathroom excuse as she was by their willingness to go on the City of the Dead tour that night. She supposed they hadn't really noticed, or cared about, her absence; it was a large, multi-room exhibit—she could have been anywhere. And she realized that they, unlike her, wouldn't be going *back* to the kirkyard.

"How did you hear about the tour?" Ellen asked.

Maggie shrugged. "I dunno. I think there was something on the TV about the kirkyard or something."

Sort of true, she thought. *The best kind of lie.*

30. Rare Books

The hours before the City of the Dead tour gave Maggie just enough time to follow up on another lead she had stumbled upon. At breakfast, after the TV had turned to other news, Maggie had overheard an interesting conversation. Nothing earth-shaking, but notable nonetheless. The front desk clerk had come in to refresh the coffee and was discussing the hotel and its environs with one of the guests. Apparently the neighborhood was undergoing a bit of a revival with eclectic shops and trendy cafés popping up. The clerk had strongly suggested the cupcake shop across from the new rare books store. Maggie had decided right then that she would have to make time to go there. Not the cupcake shop. She wasn't going to pay trendy prices for a cupcake. But a rare books store? She couldn't pass that up.

Besides, she had a hunch.

You can take the man out of the occult bookshop, but you couldn't take the occult bookshop out of the man. Or whatever. Maybe. Anyway, it was worth finding out. After all, Sarah's ghost had commanded her to find Sinclair; who was she to argue with the Spirit Realm?

So after they got back from the museum, she left Ellen and Stuart back at the hotel and walked the few short blocks to 'The

Tome Tomb.' As soon as she cross the threshold, she knew she was in the right place.

It looked identical to the interior of Sinclair's old Aberdeen store. From the stuffed floor-to-ceiling bookshelves to the dapper forty-something man standing behind the counter.

"Sinclair."

He looked up at the sound of his name. If he were surprised by her arrival, he didn't show it. "Maggie. How nice to see you again."

He looked the same as the last time she'd seen him. The second-to-last time she'd seen him had been after midnight in a graveyard with a murderer hunting them. But he held the same hard-earned self-confidence on his visage. He was dressed impeccably in beige pants and a matching silk vest, a crisp white shirt beneath. She knew, even though she couldn't see them, that his shoes were perfectly polished too. His blond goatee was still neatly trimmed and his blond hair again combed straight back. The only blemish was also the *coup de grace* to his look of controlled fury: a mottled scar running the length of his left cheek. Few people knew how he'd gotten it. Maggie was one of them.

"What happened?" Maggie got right to it. And she wasn't talking about the scar.

Sinclair hesitated. He regarded her for several seconds, his gaze seeming to penetrate her very thoughts. "Perhaps you should tell me."

Damn it. That flummoxed her. She didn't want to tell him she didn't remember anything. Apparently she didn't have to; her hesitation was enough.

"You don't remember, do you?" he probed.

"I remember enough," she rejoined.

Again he delayed his response. He raised a hand to his chin

and looked down at her, tapping his lips. "I don't think so," he finally said. "Interesting."

Maggie didn't like being examined like an ant under a magnifying glass. She knew what happened to the ant. "You know what?" she said. "Never mind. I never should have come here. I remember everything, okay? So maybe it's you who doesn't remember. What do you think of that?"

"I think," he replied, "that the more information one has the better. And you are lacking vital information."

"Yeah, well, thanks for helping with that," Maggie replied crossly. "Thanks for nothing."

Sinclair didn't say anything. He just stroked his chin and stared at her with his piercing black eyes.

Maggie decided it was time to go. In fact, she wished she'd never come. A feeling which intensified when she realized she had likely been influenced to seek him out by the fake email from the fake dead Sarah. She hated being tricked into doing things. So she was going to nip it in the bud. Now that she knew where he was, she could come back when she was ready, and on her own terms.

"Well, nice to see you," she managed to say. "I think I'll be going."

Sinclair didn't stop her. But he did watch after her, certain she'd be needing more watching after soon enough.

* * *

"And if you peer over this cubicle wall," Benson said as she finished giving Warwick a tour of Edinburgh's main precinct, "is Emma Valentine, one of our top forensic techs."

Warwick peered around, rather than over, the cubicle wall and offered Valentine a hand in greeting. "Nice to meet you."

"Likewise," Valentine replied, standing for her visitors.

"This is Sergeant Elizabeth Warwick from the Aberdeen

Police," Benson said. "She's giving us an assist on the Hotel Regency case."

"Oh really?" Valentine chimed. "I was just finishing up some more work on that one."

"What kind of work?" Warwick asked. She was always looking for more leads.

"We just finished downloading and collating all of the victim's email and social media information," Valentine answered.

Warwick rolled her eyes. She'd been doing police work long enough to remember 'little black books.' People made it so easy any more to find out everything. They posted it themselves. "Did you find anything interesting?"

"Well, we confirmed he knew that woman who killed herself up in Aberdeen. Sarah something."

"Sarah MacKenzie," Warwick said.

"Aye, that's her," Valentine replied. "They had quite the whirlwind on-line romance, it seems. That MacKenzie lass was pretty aggressive, if you know what I mean. Didn't leave much to the imagination. Lots of explicit messages. Some pretty creepy stuff too."

"Oh, really?" Benson asked, a little too curious perhaps. "Like what?"

"Well, it was kind of hard to understand," Valentine equivocated, "but if you read between the lines, I'd almost think they were into some kind of necrophilia."

"Necrophilia?" Benson repeated. She turned to Warwick. "That might explain the grave robberies."

Warwick shook her head. "I don't think so. First of all, that would make our two main suspects dead, which would be problematic. And anyway, the necrophilia cases I've done have all involved either murderers or morticians. They usually prefer fresh bodies."

Benson just stared at her for a moment. "You've done a lot of different types of cases, haven't you?"

Warwick shrugged. "I guess so."

"Well, all I know," Valentine said, "is that your Miss MacKenzie was adamant that our victim bring something she called 'the bones' when he came to Scotland. He promised to and she seemed pretty happy about, judging by the pic she sent back."

"Bones?" Benson questioned. "He couldn't have brought bones from Canada. They never would have let those through customs."

Warwick had to agree. "Maybe it's the title of a book. They were both academics."

"Aye, maybe that's it," Valentine said. "I hadn't thought of that. Too much real blood and guts in my line of work. Besides, nobody capitalizes anymore when they type, so I can't tell a book title from a necrophiliac aphrodisiac."

Benson shook her head. "Ick. I don't think I need to know any more right now."

"Oh, there's one more thing you'll be wanting to know," Valentine assured.

"What's that?" Benson replied.

"You know that grave robbery last night, at Greyfriars?" Valentine reminded them. "Well, these two mentioned Greyfriars and something about consecrating their relationship over an open grave."

Warwick looked at Benson and raised an eyebrow. They both knew where they would be going that night.

31. Bluidy MacKenzie

Later that night, after the sun had set and her blood had stopped boiling, Maggie joined Ellen and Stuart at the front gate of the darkening graveyard, preparing to enter a section so haunted it was locked *during the day*. After a brief, and suitably ominous introduction, the tour guide—a different one from the afternoon—raised his lantern and led the twenty or so tourists who'd paid for the tour into the gloom of Greyfriars Kirkyard. Maggie's big decision was whether to wait until they'd gotten inside the Covenanters Prison before peeling off and ducking into the shadows. She wasn't sure how she was going to explain this particular disappearing act, but sometimes you just had to go with a figure-out-the-excuse-later-ditch.

As it happened, they marched rather directly to the Covenanters Prison and before Maggie really had time to choose an option, the tour guide was unlocking the gate with exaggerated clanking and awe. He pushed open the cast iron gate with a long, dramatic squeak.

"Stay close," he warned, thickening his Scots brogue a bit for the tourists, "and be wary. You may sense a presence, a strange feeling, unexpected cold. These are almost to be expected any more. But if anyone experiences any injuries or sensations of being scratched or bitten, tell me immediately. The MacKenzie Poltergeist might well be in a foul mood this night."

"I don't really believe in ghosts," Stuart whispered to his companions. "Do you, Maggie?"

Maggie considered her response. She *knew* ghosts were real, so to that extent she didn't merely *believe* in them. "No," She answered.

Ellen grinned and looked at her out of the corner of her eye. "You, Maggie Devereaux, are a bonnie wee liar."

Maggie had to smile back. "You're just figuring that out?"

"Hush now," the tour guide admonished his group. Theirs wasn't the only whispered conversation.

The whispers turned from conversational to expectant. The stone walls of the prison were topped with an iron-railed walkway, from which the guards could and did shoot prisoners. Over one thousand men and boys were imprisoned there, with no shelter and a mere four ounces of bread a day, over the four months the cemetery prison was used. As the tour group moved on, a woman in the crowd suddenly spoke up.

"Did you feel that?" she asked excitedly. "Like a blast of cold air?"

"I didn't feel anything," someone replied in the dark.

"I think I did. Maybe."

"Oh, I did. Definitely."

The tour guide raised his lantern to his face. "That's Bluidy MacKenzie inspecting what he thinks are his newest prisoners. Stay calm. He's wanting to see if anyone tries to escape."

Maggie knew her cue when she heard it. As the group trudged forward, Maggie slowed to the back of the pack, then stepped behind a particularly gnarled apple tree, its wood slick, its branches empty black fingers reaching toward the sliver of the moon high in the night sky. When the group had walked far enough away, Maggie hurried over the soft, shifting ground back to the creaky iron gate. With a quick look over her shoulder to confirm no one was watching, she darted out of the Covenanters Prison. She didn't hear the people behind her.

"Did you feel that?"

"Like a rush of cold air."

"Heading right for the gate."

* * *

Maggie wasn't prepared for the almost complete blackness that blanketed the graveyard away from the tour guide's lantern. What moon there was, was thin and gave barely enough light to make out the stone path under her feet. As irritating as the darkness was, she was also thankful for it. It would give her excellent cover as she inspected the defiled grave of Rebecca NicInnes Adams.

The white-and-blue police tape stood out easily against the black of the grass and monuments. There was no cop this time. None that she saw anyway, but the thought of one made her nervous. What if he was just on break or something? She decided she didn't need to climb down into the grave or anything. Just find a quick bauble, maybe something off the headstone, even a clump of sod, then get back to the group. There was something about the whole business that was starting to give her the creeps. Like someone was watching her. It reminded her of the feeling she had in Sarah's flat. Another place that might have had its own MacKenzie Poltergeist.

She shook off the feeling and ducked under the tape. It would only take a minute. But she never got that minute. As she leaned down and patted the ground for something removable, she felt a sharp slash across her face.

"Ow!" she cried out instinctively. She immediately regretted the loud exclamation, but had no more time before the second scratch, this time across her ear, and a sudden shot of pain in her shoulder. She was overcome by a sensation of cold and the smell of something even worse than the aroma rising from the open grave.

"Ow," she couldn't help but say again, although quieter. But then a loud, "Hey!" as she felt another scratch across her throat. She tried standing to swat away whatever it was assailing her, but a final slash across the back of her head sent her tumbling off balance and into the open grave. She landed with a loud bang in a heap of stinging, dirty, ankle-sprained disarray.

She looked up from her seat atop her ancestor's rotten coffin and was relieved to feel the presence leave. She was less relieved when she realized why. A flashlight beamed down on her, blinding her until she shaded her eyes against it.

"Maggie Devereaux?" the flashlight-wielder asked.

Maggie recognized the voice. *Damn.* She looked up and offered a smile. "Hello, Sergeant Warwick."

32. You Have the Right to Remain Silent

The Edinburgh police station was actually rather pleasant. It was well lit, with a comfortable lobby and walls covered in a genial combination of art and historical photographs. If it hadn't been for the fact that it was the middle of the night, her friends didn't know where she was, and she was locked into an interrogation room, Maggie might actually have liked the place.

She lowered her head into her hands and waited for her inquisitor to arrive. At least they'd taken off the handcuffs. But as she sat there, tired, mind racing, a little hungry, and generally miserable, she knew they were making her wait to add to her discomfort. One more way to crack her. But it didn't matter. She was never, ever going to tell them the truth, so they could do whatever they wanted. It's not like she actually knew anything anyway.

She looked up at the corner of the room. There was a completely-not-disguised video camera pointed right at her, its red recording light blinking. *Great,* she thought, returning her head to her hands. Her humiliation would be memorialized for posterity. How could it get worse?

The door opened. It got worse.

Sergeant Warwick walked in. Inspector Benson was right

behind her.

"Hello, Maggie," Warwick said as she sat down opposite her. Benson remained standing. "You're in a lot of trouble."

Maggie knew that was probably true, but she wasn't sure what law she had actually broken. Maybe trespassing, but that couldn't be that big of a deal. Plus, she could always claim she was attacked by the ghost of Bluidy George MacKenzie. "For what?" she challenged them.

"For what?!" Benson echoed incredulously. "Tampering with a crime scene, for starters."

Ah, okay. That was more serious than just trespassing. "I wasn't tampering. I fell in."

"You ducked under the crime scene tape, Maggie," Warwick pointed out. "It's not like you were just on a stroll and suddenly fell into an open grave."

"Would you believe me," Maggie tried, "if I said I was being chased by the MacKenzie Poltergeist?"

"No, we wouldn't," Benson answered.

But Warwick didn't answer Maggie's question. Instead, she asked another of her own. "The City of the Dead tour is on the other side of the kirkyard. Why were you over by the grave?"

Maggie wasn't sure how to respond.

"What's your interest in that grave, Maggie?" Warwick pressed. "You can tell me."

Maggie almost believed she could. But not with Benson standing there. And not with the video camera on.

"Returning to the scene of the crime," Benson suggested. "Like when we caught you sneaking out of Sarah MacKenzie's flat."

"What?" Maggie looked up at the tall policewoman. "There was no crime there. She committed suicide."

"So you admit you went inside?" Benson demanded.

"I never said that," Maggie replied quickly. She was pretty sure she hadn't said that. She'd done it, but she hadn't said it.

"Don't play dumb, Devereaux," Benson warned. "We know you weren't out for a walk that night with that bloke, what was his name?"

"Philip." Maggie was keen to solidify her alibi. "Philip Harmon. He's a visiting professor at the college. And I most certainly did go for a walk with him that night." *Although it was after* he *rescued me from you two.*

"Why did you go inside the flat?" Warwick asked evenly, almost conversationally.

Maggie narrowed her eyes at Warwick. How much had they seen?

"We found your fingerprints inside the flat," Benson asserted.

Maggie was pretty sure that was a bluff. They would need samples of her fingerprints to make a match, wouldn't they? And the one time she'd ever been fingerprinted, she'd seen to it they didn't last in police custody. Still, maybe they lifted them off a can she threw in the recycling or something.

"Well, Sarah was my faculty advisor," Maggie explained. "So if my fingerprints are in there, it's probably because I touched something once when I visited her."

Maggie thought that was a pretty good explanation. Benson's frustrated expression confirmed it.

"Maggie." Warwick leaned forward earnestly. "You need to cut the bravado and start being honest."

Do you even know how to be honest? Maggie could hear Iain's mocking voice.

"I am being honest," Maggie asserted. "I wasn't doing anything wrong. I don't know anything. I don't even know why I'm here."

"You're here," Benson barked, "because you're connected to three different crime scenes. Apparently separate crimes, except for the fact that you're tied to all three."

"Me?" Maggie was taken aback by the accusation. Then she thought about it for a moment. Sarah's flat... Greyfriars... And... "Three?" she asked.

Benson glared at her for a moment, then pulled Maggie's pendant from her pocket and shoved it in her face. "Three."

Reflexively, Maggie reached up to her naked neck. She damned herself for doing so. They all knew what it meant.

"This is your pendant, isn't it?" Benson demanded.

Maggie didn't answer.

"It was found at a murder scene here in Edinburgh," Warwick explained, decidedly more calmly than Benson would have. Warwick was obviously the good cop. *Good choice*, Maggie thought. She liked Warwick. Benson not so much. "The murder was similar to the ones at the college last fall, right after you arrived. We're going to take your fingerprints and DNA tonight, Maggie. Our forensics team found female DNA at the scene. If it's yours, you're looking at a lot more than just tampering with a crime scene."

Maggie sat there, trying to think of some plausible lie as to why her DNA would be in that hotel room. But she couldn't think of anything. She still didn't know the real reason she was in that hotel room.

"What do you have to say for yourself, Maggie?" Warwick asked.

Maggie shook her head. She was all out of explanations. "Do I have the right to remain silent?"

Warwick frowned, but nodded. "Yes."

"Then, yeah, I'm going to do that. Silent. Me. Now." Then, feeling a little rude, she added, "Thanks."

"No, thank you," Benson replied. "Now we can arrest you."

"Arrest me?" Maggie exclaimed. "For what?"

"We told you," Benson answered. "Tampering with a crime scene. Maybe trespassing too. And I bet we can think of more before your arraignment tomorrow morning."

"Arraignment?" Maggie was stunned. "You're really arresting me? I'm really going to jail?"

"I'm afraid so, Maggie," Warwick answered. "Unless you want to stay here and tell us the truth."

Maggie knew that wasn't really an option. She just looked down at the table and shook her head.

"Good." Benson knocked on the door and a large uniformed officer stepped into the room. He fastened handcuffs back onto Maggie and led her out of the room.

"You better hope your prints aren't on that pendant, Devereaux," Benson shouted after her.

"Don't worry," Maggie muttered to herself, the magic seething behind her caramel eyes. "They won't be."

33. Small Time Criminal

At least she didn't have to worry about nightmares. She was too scared to sleep.

They put her in a 'pod' with seven other women. They all seemed tough and mean and dirty and scary. But they left her alone. It was after 'lights out' when she was brought in and everyone just wanted to sleep. So except for a couple of introductions and a 'Whattaya in for?' they pretty much ignored her. Maggie realized they all had their own problems already.

The next morning, after a breakfast ironically more appealing and satisfying than the one at the hotel, she was taken to court. Sort of. She was taken to a small room in the jail with a video hook-up to the actual courtroom, out there somewhere else. A magistrate in a white wig and black robe was on the screen. Maggie was still in her orange jail pajamas and rubber slip-on shoes. She was guided by the guard to a chair next to remarkably young-looking attorney, also wearing a powdered wig. If it hadn't been so serious, it would have been ridiculous.

"Hello," he said, barely looking up from his large stack of files. He had a neatly trimmed black beard and, just visible beneath the wig, small gauges in his earlobes. "I'm Tim. I'm the public defender this morning."

"Oh, okay." Maggie wasn't sure what to say. She was still in shock to find herself where she was just then.

"I have good news," Tim said. "You're being bound over."

That didn't sound good. "What does that mean?"

"I talked with the prosecutor this morning," Tim replied. "They aren't really too concerned about a little trespassing, especially in a public graveyard. He said something about their lab having trouble with some fingerprinting they tried to rush through. I convinced them to hold off charging you and to release you on your promise to appear in the future."

Maggie felt an ocean of relief wash over her. "That's it? I can go home?"

"You can go home," Tim confirmed, "but that's not it. You'll be fingerprinted, and they'll swab the inside of your cheek for DNA. And you'll have to surrender your passport. Then you have to come back to court in two weeks, on November first. You may be charged at that time and taken back into custody. And if you try to leave the U.K., you'll be arrested."

Maggie needed a moment for all of that to sink in. "Well, crap. But thanks."

Tim shrugged and pulled the next file from his stack. "Glad to have helped." Then he finally looked directly at her—and winked. "Good luck with whatever the blazes you're doing."

Maggie smiled. If only he knew how right he was.

34. Canadian Know-Who

The police had a head start on Maggie back to Aberdeen. It took several hours before she was actually given her clothes back and released from the jail—after they extracted fingerprints and DNA from her. She'd thought having a burly cop grab her hands and press each of her fingers onto an ink pad and print card was humiliating, until they'd shoved a giant Q-tip into her mouth and scraped the inside of her cheeks for her DNA.

Once she was out in the sunlight again, she had to trudge back to the hotel. Ellen had been worried sick all night. Stuart had apparently been the shoulder to cry on. *Great. Insult to injury.* Maggie explained that it was all a big misunderstanding, but said little more. She just wanted to get home. By the time they checked out and were on the road to Aberdeen, Sgt. Warwick was knocking on the door of Philip Harmon's flat.

Warwick was glad to be back in Aberdeen. Sinclair hadn't been especially helpful. He hadn't been truthful either, she knew, but that would take time to unravel. The appearance of Maggie Devereaux had been disconcerting. Warwick had no doubt the young American was wrapped up in it all somehow. She also had no doubt Maggie wasn't the culprit. But Maggie's appearance in the case made Warwick uncomfortable. She had a file cabinet with a drawer reserved for her unsolved cases. There was only one file in it and it too had Maggie Devereaux wrapped up in it. She didn't want to add a second file to that drawer.

Luckily, Maggie had given them a name. Philip Harmon. And unlike Devan Sinclair, Philip Harmon had made no efforts to conceal his whereabouts.

He opened the door just before Warwick was about to knock again. "Hello?" he greeted her.

"Hello." She displayed her badge. "I'm Sergeant Elizabeth Warwick of the Aberdeen Police." Then to make sure he was uncomfortable, and therefore pliable. "I believe we've met before."

Philip's eyes widened just a bit. It was one thing to act brave in front of an attractive young lady you were trying to impress. It was quite another thing when the cop came back and knocked on your door. "Oh. Yes. Right. Of course." He opened his door all the way. "Please come in."

Warwick stepped in and surveyed the small residence. It was decorated sparsely. Just a few photographs on top of some of the flat surfaces. There were some unpacked boxes still in the corner.

"I haven't unfinished packing yet," Philip apologized. "Those boxes just arrived from Canada. I didn't expect to be staying quite so long. I just found this flat a few weeks ago. I'm talking too much. Sorry. Would you like some tea?"

Warwick shook her head and smiled slightly. He was a nervous one. "No, thank you." She sat down in a small chair in the sitting area. Philip followed suit, sitting on the small couch opposite the coffee table. "So," she followed up, "you didn't expect to be staying in Aberdeen? What changed?"

"Ah, yes, well." Philip was wringing his hands. Warwick supposed he didn't talk to the police much. Most decent people didn't. "I was only in Scotland on vacation—'holiday' as you call it. A two-week trip. I hadn't even planned on visiting Aberdeen. No offense, but I was planning on Edinburgh and Glasgow, then Loch Ness, of course." He smiled weakly.

"Of course," Warwick replied. "And none taken. Sounds like a typical tourist trip across Scotland."

"Exactly."

"So what happened?"

"A phone call. Just as I was leaving Edinburgh, I got a call from my university. Apparently the college up here had been expecting a visiting professor from my same university but he, well, he met an untimely demise—"

"I think I'm aware," Warwick interjected.

Philip seemed surprised, then nodded. "Right. Of course. Why wouldn't you be? Well, yes, so Aberdeen contacted my university and they knew I was already here. They made a few calls and next thing I know I'm driving up to Aberdeen to take over his assignment. I really couldn't pass up an opportunity to teach in Scotland for a year."

Warwick nodded. "So, in a way, you benefited from his murder."

Philip raised his eyebrows, then exhaled loudly. "Well, I never really thought of it like that." He shrugged. "But I suppose that's right, in a way."

"So you were in Edinburgh when the murder occurred?" Warwick confirmed.

Philip nodded. "I believe so. I learned about it later, of course. As I said, I never made it to Glasgow or Loch Ness. I came straight here from Edinburgh, so I must have been there when it happened."

Warwick nodded. She had a few more areas to cover, but

she wanted to keep it brief. He'd given her a pretty complicated story. It would be easy enough to see if any part of it didn't check out, and if didn't, she'd be back. On to the next subject. She pulled out some photographs from her purse and laid one of them on the coffee table.

"Do you recognize this woman?"

Philip stared at the picture for several seconds. He rubbed his chin. Warwick wondered were his uncertainty lay: whether he recognized the person, or whether to tell her that he did. Finally, he said, "I believe that's Sarah MacKenzie. She was a professor here at the college. I was told she committed suicide this summer. I saw some newspaper clippings in the faculty lounge."

Warwick nodded again. He'd gotten the ID right. She wondered whether the rest of the story was true. She placed a second photo onto the table. It was Derek Peabody's driver's license photo. A photo from the bathtub would have given it away.

Philip stared at this one too, chin in hand, but he was much quicker to assert, "No, I don't recognize him at all."

The denial seemed a bit swift to Warwick, but not overly so, but if he'd recognized Sarah MacKenzie from a newspaper in the faculty lounge, wouldn't he know his own colleague from Canada? Then again, Peabody wasn't in the newspaper for killing himself.

She laid the third and final photo on the table. They both knew he recognized this one. Warwick wondered if he'd be smart enough to say so.

Thoughts raced unexpressed behind Philip's eyes. Then a smile unfolded. "Well, of course I know her. That's Maggie Devereaux. The woman I rescued from your clutches the other night."

Smart man, Warwick thought.

"Of course," he added, "I didn't realize at the time that you were the police, or just how serious a matter this was. I could just see that Maggie was uncomfortable so I came to the rescue."

Warwick wasn't sure she believed that, but she appreciated the effort to explain away his interference with their investigation.

"Did you know," Warwick asked as she gathered up the photos, "that we were all standing right on front of Sarah MacKenzie's former flat?"

"Were you?" Philip expressed surprise. "No, I didn't know that."

"How do you know Maggie?" Warwick asked.

Again a pause as gears turned behind his eyes. "Well, primarily because she's a student at the college and I met her on one of my first days. In fact, now that I think about it, she'd come looking for Sarah MacKenzie, and they'd given me her old office."

"You know, I was there when a friend of hers told her about Professor MacKenzie. She seemed quite surprised." He thought for a moment, then added, "Although I don't know why she would be. I've come to learn that it was pretty common knowledge. Pretty shocking news on a university campus."

Interesting point, Warwick conceded. But there was another point in his previous answer that she didn't want to just let go by. "You said 'primarily.' How else do you know her?"

Philip frowned. "Well, now that you've asked me all these questions and I'm thinking about it..." but he trailed off.

"Yes?" Warwick prompted. She handed him Maggie's photo again.

"Well, it's just that—" He stared at the photo, then looked up. "Well, I'm pretty sure I saw her in Edinburgh at the time of the murder."

35. Looking Backward

October was flying by. Samhain had almost arrived. Ellen had hoped to plan some sort of party for the 31st, but when she found out Maggie might be going to Callanish with Philip, she quickly dropped her plans and made an uncomfortable remark about parting the veils.

Maggie still thought of it as 'might be going' even though she had told Philip she would. Something was holding her back from fully committing to it. She told herself it was something to do with her missing book and the mystery she found herself wrapped up in. But she knew it was something else.

No emails. No voicemails. Nothing.

Stupid Iain.

* * *

A week before Halloween/Samhain found Maggie at yet another coffee shop near campus. This one was called 'The Gear Grinder' and was decorated in a sort of neo-goth, steampunk motif. Maggie wasn't really sure what steampunk was—other than trendy—but most of the decorations boasted gears, lenses, leather, and/or brass. It all worked somehow and the atmosphere was both edgy and comfortable. The coffee wasn't bad either. But that's not why she chose that particular coffee shop. She chose it because it had the most outlets in the walls, and she was going to need to be able to plug her laptop in. She had some research to do and some plans to make.

She ordered a grandé latte and found a table in the back. She fired up her laptop then began extracting the things she'd brought in her backpack. A print-out of an article about the Greyfriars Kirkyard grave robbery. The genealogy her grandmother had done, connecting Maggie thirteen generations back to Brìghde Innes. And a map of Scotland. She had a hunch, and she'd learned to listen to her hunches.

Someone had dug up one of her ancestors. The news mentioned it was one of a rash of such grave robberies across Scotland. It didn't take a rocket scientist to guess there was connection. But it might take a witch to know what the connection was. She took a sip of her coffee and opened her browser.

There had been seven grave robberies so far; the most recent being Rebecca Adams from Greyfriars. The news reports of the grave robberies varied in quantity and quality of details. They all included the names of the bodies, though. And while they generally only provided the first and last names, Maggie knew they all shared the same middle name: NicInnes, 'Daughter of Innes.' Just like her.

She checked off the names on her genealogy. There was no mistaking it. Someone was digging up her ancestors. That was bad. But they were going in reverse order, and they weren't done yet. That was good. She knew where they were going to strike next.

Maggie read the entry aloud. "Catrìona NicInnes Ramsay, daughter of Margaret NicInnes Wilkie." Margaret the Witch, buried outside the kirkyard fence at the Castle of Park. "Born 1647. Died 1726. Buried at St. James cemetery in Ayrsduff, Cromartyshire."

Maggie turned to the map. Cromartyshire was way up on the northwest coast, across The Minch from the Isle of Lewis and

Callanish. In addition, it was deep in the Highland *Gàidhealtachd* where the daily language was still Gaelic. She smiled for that. It had been too long since she'd spoken a little *Gàidhlig*. But the smile faded as she realized something. If they were working backwards, had they already struck the two most recent generations? Had they somehow already defiled the New World graves of her grandmother and mother?

She quickly surfed over to the news sites for Seattle. Sites for the TV stations like KING-5 and KIRO, and the newspapers like The Seattle Times and The Post-Intelligencer. She didn't find anything, but that didn't convince her nothing had happened. Seattle was a big city; a couple of random grave robberies might not have warranted much of a story. And if the culprits had indeed started there, the crimes would have happened so long ago, those stories would already be archived.

Indeed, they would have happened during The Lost Weeks. She thought she could have expected at least an email from her dad if something had happened to her mom's grave. But all the emails from those weeks were gone—or were they deleted? Should she email her dad? What if it hadn't happened? He didn't always like to talk about her mom; it hurt too much. What would an email do that started, 'Hey, has anyone dug up mom's body recently?'

She frowned and tapped her lips. The news reports said whoever was doing this was removing body parts from the coffins. So, if someone had done this back in the States, would they have brought some sort of body parts with them? How could they possibly have made it through customs? Did she know anyone who'd just arrived from the U.S.? No. But she knew someone who'd just arrived from next door to the U.S. Next door to Seattle, even.

Philip.

But then she remembered how he'd saved her from the

police outside Sarah's flat. No, she decided she could trust him. Somehow, she knew that.

Which left the other Canadian—the one in the bathtub, covered in blood. The one whose blood was also in Sarah's flat. Had he brought something? Or had he failed and that had been his punishment?

She decided several things. First, it didn't look like her mother's and grandmother's graves had been bothered. Second, it didn't matter if they had, because regardless, the next victim would be Catrìona in Ayrsduff. Third, she needed another ride, and it was *not* going to involve Stuart Menzies.

Before she could decide anything else, her 'new email' tone rang. It startled, and worried, her enough that she didn't notice the person who had just walked into the café. She hesitated, but then decided that she had completed enough on her ancestor quest that even if the email was what she feared, and it completely derailed her train of thought, she was in the right depot already. She clicked the email icon and up popped her 'in' box.

Sure enough, it was right at the top. The latest missive from sarah123@scotmail.com. The subject line was 'Next Steps.' Maggie found it particularly irritating that Sarah MacKenzie's ghost was going to tell her what her next steps should be right after she had just decided on them herself. She glared at the email for a few seconds, then opened it.

The Dark Book is safe as long as you stop looking for it. But I know you and I know what you're doing. Stop now if you value your own life.

"Oh, my God, Maggie!" came the shout behind her. It was Ellen, reading over her shoulder, her hands covering her agape mouth. "What's going on?"

"Ellen!" Maggie spun around to face her friend. She folded her laptop shut, but it was too late. "What are you doing here?"

"Never mind that," Ellen nearly shrieked. "What was that email?"

Maggie's heart and mind were both racing. "What email?" she tried. It didn't work.

"The one you just slammed shut." Ellen pointed at the laptop. "The one that threatened your life."

Maggie glanced back at her computer. "I'm not sure it was threat exactly."

Ellen threw herself down in the chair next to Maggie. "What's going on, Mags? Are you in some kind of trouble?"

What's going on? Maggie repeated in her mind. Where could she even begin? The back-story would fill a novel, maybe two. And Ellen would never believe it anyway. Still, she could hardly just deny everything. Ellen had just read the email. But she could try to limit it to that subject.

"I've been getting some strange emails," Maggie admitted. "From someone I don't know. I'm not really sure what they're supposed to mean. I'm not too worried about it, though."

"Are they just spam?" Ellen asked. "Or are they specific to you? What's the Dark Book? Is that something you know about?"

"Uh, yeah, they're pretty specific," Maggie answered. She avoided a direct response about the Dark Book.

"How many have you gotten?"

"Um, three or four, I think."

"Who are they from?"

Maggie shrugged. "I don't know."

Ellen frowned. "Well, what's the email address?"

Maggie shook her head. This wasn't going to help soothe

Ellen. "It's sarah123@scotmail.com."

"Oh, my God!" Ellen did shriek this time. "You're getting emails from Sarah MacKenzie's ghost?!"

Maggie ignored the other customers who'd turned to look back at their table. "I highly doubt it," she replied. "It's probably just somebody playing a joke on me."

"It's cyber-stalking is what it is," Ellen retorted. "That's a crime. Have you called the police?"

Maggie grimaced. She'd had enough of the police lately. "No. I don't really want to get the police involved."

Ellen cocked her head at Maggie's tone, but didn't challenge her. Instead, she thought for a moment, then said, "Well, there are other ways to find out what's going on."

Maggie allowed a small smile. "Oh yeah?" She definitely wanted to find out what was going on.

"Aye," Ellen replied. "Stuart has a friend. A real computer whiz. I bet he could figure out who's really sending you those emails. All that stuff can be tracked, if you know how to do it."

"Which I don't," Maggie admitted.

"Me either," Ellen said. "But Stuart's friend, Dougie, does. I'm sure he could do it. And Stuart will do anything I ask him to."

Maggie frowned. "I'm sure," she groaned.

Ellen frowned too, but it was still friendly. "I know he's not the best-looking lad ever. He's a bit thin, and pale. And he probably only starting talking to me because he figured out I was friends with that cute American girl he saw at the library, but he's really not so bad, Mags. He was honestly worried when you went missing on that cemetery tour. He said he felt like it was his fault."

"His fault?" Maggie questioned. Interesting.

"Well, like I said," Ellen replied, "he's a nice lad. A bit sensitive maybe. But back to the point, he'll do anything to help me, and probably more to help you. He'll get Dougie to do it."

Maggie shook her head. "Thanks, but I don't need help," she insisted.

Ellen clicked her tongue at Maggie. "Now, now. Didn't you tell Iain you wanted someone you could trust? Someone you could count on to help you?"

Maggie shrugged. "I'm not sure that's exactly what I said."

"Close enough," Ellen grinned. "Let me take your computer. I'll give it to Dougie and I'm sure he can figure out who's sending you those nasty emails."

Maggie frowned again and considered the offer. Finally, she opened her laptop again and started clicking things. "Okay, fine," she relented. "You can take it. I'm not going to need it for a few days anyway."

Ellen beamed. "Brilliant. I'm so happy you agreed, I won't even ask why you won't need it." She looked at her friend for a moment. "But I will ask what you're doing right now."

"Deleting my browsing history," Maggie answered. "I don't want Dougie, or Stuart, or even you, to see everything I do on my computer."

Ellen shook her head and laughed. "Always the mysterious one, eh?"

Maggie smiled. "It's in my blood."

36. Ayrsduff

The village of Ayrsduff—meaning 'dark coast,' from the Gaelic *earre*, for coast, and *dubh*, dark—was on the northwest coast of Scotland, approximately halfway between the Hebrides and nowhere, and accessible only by a single road which was both narrow enough not to allow two cars to pass in opposite directions and desolate enough for that not to matter. Maggie had needed a ride, and needed to only ask once, receiving an immediate and emphatic, "Yes!" Now she found herself riding shotgun through the deepest part of the Highlands in a subcompact hastily rented by one Philip Harmon.

She'd mentioned the *Gàidhealtachd* of course, but she supposed (and hoped) that her own company might also have been a selling point. They motored along, a bit slower than really necessary as Philip got used to driving on the wrong side of the treacherously narrow road.

"Doesn't this sort of remind you of the Cascade foothills?" Philip asked, pointing to the grassy, rolling landscape.

Maggie looked around. Philip was right; it did look a bit like the hills that gathered at the base of the Cascade Mountains east of Seattle—and Vancouver, she supposed. "It sure does," she agreed. "Although they're covered in pine trees near Seattle."

"Right," Philip nodded. "Up by Vancouver too. And you can see the actual snow-covered peaks in the background."

Maggie regarded their current horizon. Nothing but slate gray sky behind the rolling mini-mountains. It gave the illusion of water being perpetually over the next hill, but Maggie knew from the map that they still had at least an hour before they'd reach Ayrsduff. She wondered if Philip had the same sensation. But before she could ask, she realized that Iain, instead of sharing her observations and feelings, would have been telling her all the things she *didn't* notice, invoking feeling she didn't know to have. It was nice to be with someone like herself, but she missed who she could become when she was with someone different from herself.

Stupid Iain.

She sighed, a little too loudly.

Philip glanced over at her, but only momentarily, his eyes glued to the twisting ribbon of road. "You okay?"

She frowned from the window and smiled to her reflection. "Yeah, sure. It's just... something about the landscape, I guess. I'm just feeling kinda quiet. I think I'll just look at the scenery for a bit."

Philip nodded. "No worries. I understand. I'll wake you if I drive off the road."

Maggie chuckled despite her melancholy. "I'm sure that would wake me. Thanks, Philip."

He didn't reply. Which was perfect.

* * *

By the time they reached their destination, it matched its name. The sun was beginning its descent into the North Atlantic, swelling orange beyond the waters of The Minch and Isle of Lewis. Long shadows lined the small town, which would have needed an influx of residents to even warrant being called a village. There were a handful of one-story houses scattered around the main central buildings: the pub (of course), the church, and the hotel. The town cemetery, Maggie was sure to note, was behind the church.

The hotel was the only building more than two stories, although only barely. At three stories, it was the tallest structure in the town save the church steeple. It was a simple building, with wooden clapboard painted a dirtying white. Its only windows were in front, all facing the water. Above the door hung a simple sign, red with white letters: *TAIGH-ÒSDA*. Gaelic for 'hotel.'

"Well, look at that." Philip slapped his knee. "We really are in a *Gàidhealtachd*, aren't we?"

"*Tha*," Maggie replied affirmatively in Gaelic. "<We're in a *Gàidhealtachd*.>'

Then she grinned and raised an eyebrow. "<Gaelic only?>" she challenged.

"Oh, I don't know." He laughed nervously. "Er, that is... <I'm not certainty. I am never has been on a *Gàidhealtachd* earlier.>"

Maggie laughed. "Close," she said in English. "You just need some practice." She made a sweeping gesture at the small town. "No better place than this."

Philip nodded. "Okay," he agreed. "<I am be trying.>"

Maggie smiled at the awkward syntax, then shook her head at the irony of finding a fellow Gaelic speaker from Canada, rather than a certain handsome Scot who used to drive her around the entire kingdom but didn't speak a word of his nation's ancestral tongue. Her previous melancholy at the thought of Iain was tempered by the rush she always got when got to speak another language—especially Gaelic.

They parked the car directly in front of the hotel and walked inside. The entry was more living room than hotel lobby, with a reception desk pushed against a far wall on the other side of a sitting area with four stuffed chairs by a fireplace. A dining room was visible on the other side of a central staircase, with a door to the kitchen beyond that. Lots of dark wood and embroidered fabric. Cozy. Definitely a B&B vibe.

Maggie smiled. *Nice.*

She stepped to one side and pushed Philip gently toward the woman bent over the reception desk. "<Gaelic,>" she reminded him.

He sighed, but then offered a smile and nodded.

The woman stood up to greet them. She was large. Large all around. Tall, heavy set, with lots of layers of clothes and a barely tamed mane of brown and gray hair loose around her head and down her back. She wore wire-rimmed glasses at the end of her pink nose, and an assortment of jewelry, from rings to bracelets to multiple earrings, jingled as she extended a hand and stepped over to them.

"*Fàilte,*" she said. Gaelic for 'welcome.' She didn't follow up with the English too, like they did in some of the more southern *Gàidhealtachds,* to give the guest the option of which language to respond in. This was Gaelic only. Maggie crossed her arms and smiled, eager to watch the show.

"Uh, hallo," Philip started uneasily. "<We will be to stay here two days ago.>"

The woman raised an eyebrow. "<Excuse me?>"

Philip frowned, eyes narrowing in concentration. "<Uh, our desires make us in need of a room right now.>"

This time both eyebrows shot up. A bemused smile played across her lips. She looked to Maggie.

Maggie shook her head, but decided she better step in before Philip got them kicked out of the only hotel in town.

"<Sorry,>" she began. "<My friend's Gaelic is a bit rusty. We would like two rooms, please. We'll be staying two nights.>"

"<Ah,>" the woman said. "<I guessed it was something like

that.>" She paused and looked at Philip, who was not altogether unhandsome despite his flailing language skills. "<Two rooms, you say? Not one?>"

"<No, two,>" Maggie was clear. "<Thank you.>"

The woman approvingly looked at Philip again, then turned to fetch two room keys off the punchboard behind her.

"Two rooms, eh?" Philip whispered to Maggie in English. "I understood that much."

Maggie didn't reply, save a beguiling smile. Once she switched to Gaelic, she didn't like to switch back.

The woman returned and handed them their keys. "<My name is Rhona. If you need anything at all, just ask. I hope you enjoy your stay.>"

"*Tapadh leibh*," Maggie thanked her.

"*Tapadh leibh*," Philip parroted, grateful to be able to fire off the rote phrase for 'thank you.'

They stepped outside to fetch their bags, but Maggie suddenly grabbed his arm and pulled him toward the street. "<Let's go for a walk,>" she said, sticking with her Gaelic. He might not be able to speak it fluently, but she knew he understood it when it was spoken to him.

Philip took a moment to confirm what he'd heard, then another to reply. "<All right. That has the ring of being something that is good.>"

Maggie shook her head amicably. He needed the trip almost more than she did. Almost. She wasn't just dragging him along on some romantic sunset walk—not just. She was also running reconnaissance. They were walking toward the church, and behind it, the cemetery.

"So," Philip seemed embarrassed to say, "can we speak English now? My Gaelic is humiliatingly inadequate."

"<What's that?>" Maggie teased. "<I'm sorry. I don't understand English.>"

Philip grimaced. "This is going to be an awkward conversation if we're each speaking a different language."

"Okay, okay," Maggie finally relented. "You can have a little *Beurla* if you want"—the Gaelic word for 'English'—"but you're never going to get better if you don't practice."

"I have every intention of practicing my Gaelic," Philip insisted. "Later. When I have to."

"Fine." Maggie bumped into him playfully. "But you better keep me around in case you get into trouble."

Philip nodded and smiled at her. "I'd like nothing more."

Maggie felt a blush starting. She coughed and looked away. "Yes, well, hmm..."

Philip was smart enough to move the conversation on a bit. "So, why did we come here again?"

Maggie was glad for the change of topic. "Oh, just some research," she answered without much thought. It was her standard response.

"Oh, yeah?" Philip replied. "On what?"

Oh, crap. Maggie realized she and Philip probably did a lot of the same research. He'd actually be interested in whatever it was she was doing. So much for the comfort of being with someone like herself. She was definitely uncomfortable all of a sudden. "Er, uh... It's kind of a secret."

Lame, Devereaux, she knew.

Philip frowned. "I'm not going to steal your ideas, Maggie."

Maggie's heart sank. She knew that, of course. In fact, she hadn't even considered it, which was why she'd gone ahead and said what she'd said. Iain would have just accepted the 'secret' reply. Hell, he would have let it go after the 'research' explanation.

But Philip took it completely differently. Rather than a chance for unspoken trust, it had exploded in her hands, a statement of competitive distress. *Damn.*

She looked ahead. They were almost to the cemetery. She knew how to get to it. That was good enough for now.

"<Come on>," she said, switching back to Gaelic and turning around. "<We should go back. It's getting dark.>"

* * *

Dinner started as a quiet affair. There was allegedly another guest at the hotel, but she had apparently gone to the pub for the evening. Maggie expected she and Philip would eat at the pub too, but when they'd gotten back from their walk, Rhona had made some cryptic comment about being relieved they were back before dark. Cryptic, but concerned. Maggie knew there was information behind the sentiment, so she decided to find out what it was, over dinner at the hotel with Rhona. Philip was surprised and tried to talk Maggie into going out to the pub after all, but he soon learned that in addition to being more than a wee bit mysterious, Maggie was more than a wee bit stubborn.

He gave in without too much of a fight and soon they sat down for a dinner of baked fish and sautéed potatoes. It took almost no effort at all to convince Rhona to join them after she'd brought out the food, and Maggie began her interrogation. It was disguised as simple tourist curiosity and was, to Philip's chagrin, entirely in Gaelic.

Maggie had information to gather. Philip would just have to keep up.

The conversation started with the usual chit-chat. When the city was founded. Some high points of local history. A couple of the more famous residents. The importance of the distant town as a haven of Gaelic language and culture during The Clearances.

Eventually, though, after dinner was eaten and they were onto the whisky, it was time to get to the point.

"<So, an old town like this,>" Maggie took a sip from her glass, "<must have some good ghost stories.>"

"<Oh, aye,>" answered Rhona. Philip was just squinting at the two women over his glass, his face fixed in concentration, as it had been all dinner, as he listened to their rapidly spoken Gaelic. "<Ayrsduff has a long history of ghosts and magic. One of our more famous residents was herself reputed to be a witch.>"

"<You don't say,>" Maggie feigned surprise. "<Who was that then?>"

"<Catrìona Ramsay,>" Rhona confirmed. "<She moved here when she was an old woman. Her family stayed back south, but she wanted to get away and be free to practice her family's arts.>"

"<What kind of arts?>" Maggie asked. "<Not the Dark Arts?>"

"<No, child. The White Arts.>" Rhona nodded and poured them both some more whisky. "<Legend was, they burned Catrìona's mother as a witch, but there were no witches in that family. They were healers and soothsayers. They weren't in league with demons. They fought against them.>"

"<Did they?>" Maggie was glad to hear that. But she wouldn't mind some confirmation. "<How do you know that?>"

"<Because she's still fighting them,>" Rhona answered. "<They dug up her body just last night.>"

37. A Midsummer Night's Jog

Nightfall couldn't come fast enough for Maggie. Or rather, that time several hours after nightfall when she was pretty sure everyone in the hotel, especially Philip, was asleep. But it came, eventually, and Maggie cracked open her door to peek into the hallway.

There was no one about. A single table lamp at the end of the hallway lit the walkway in a yellow glow. She stepped out, dressed all in black, holding a black flashlight, and—in what she thought might be a bit of overkill—wearing a black knit cap on her head. She looked every bit the burglar. Or grave robber. She closed the door behind her with the faintest of bumps and turned the old-fashioned skeleton key to lock it. It clicked louder than she might have liked, especially in the otherwise silent hotel, but she didn't think it wise to leave her room unlocked. Who knew what kind of weirdoes might be out lurking that night?

Despite her best efforts, each step managed to find a creaky floorboard to announce her journey from her room to the top of the stairs. The steps were even worse.

Creak. Creak. Creeeeeak.

She was sure she must be waking up everyone in the hotel. All three of them. But she made it to the door without anyone suddenly turning on a light and asking where in the world she thought she was going at that hour. Another open and close of a door and she was outside in the cool night air. Cold, actually, that far north on the coast in October. She was glad she'd gone with the hat after all.

The earlier walk with Philip quickly proved its value. It was dark as Hell outside. Well, actually, she didn't suppose Hell was all that dark—not with all that fire and everything—but it sure was dark in Ayrsduff. There were absolutely no streetlights and every light in every building was off. Even the pub. She wondered whether anyone was awake at all. Did they even have a fire station or a police station? It sure didn't look like it. The only lights in the whole town came from a weak moon behind some unhelpfully thick clouds, and Maggie's flashlight. She shined it ahead of her and hurried to the graveyard.

But when she got there, she began to regret not having gone on a longer walk with Philip. She stood at the gate of the cemetery—a waist-high iron-bar affair—but realized she didn't know where Catrìona's grave might be. She had supposed it would be a small graveyard. It was a small town after all, but it was an old town and a lot of people had died there over the centuries. Finding a single grave out of a hundred with only a flashlight was going to be slow work. Not to mention more than a little eerie.

She lifted the latch on the gate with a disquieting creak and pushed it open with an even more ominous one. Not that there was anyone around to hear it. Just her and a graveyard full of flesh-eating zombies. Fighting off a shudder, she stepped into the cemetery.

It was perfectly quiet. The only sounds were the very distant crash of waves against the shore and the very near squelching of her shoes on the wet grass. It was slippery and the earth shifted sometimes under her feet. She pointed her flashlight directly in front of her, lest she trip on a headstone, but she also needed to sweep the beam around the cemetery, searching for the open grave, unless she was prepared to step over every square inch of the grounds, flashlight straight down, until she came across it.

She expected the defiled grave should be easy enough to spot, if only because of the large pile of dirt that would be next to it. Maybe even some crime scene tape like in Edinburgh, although she wasn't convinced Ayrsduff even had a police force. There'd been no sign of it yet. She walked carefully forward, alternating between sweeping the area for dirt piles and checking her feet for tripping hazards.

As she got deeper into the cemetery, she began to notice trees that blocked both her view and her path. It was getting hazardous quickly. She needed to find that grave.

The next swing of the beam revealed a dark form that could have been, maybe, a pile of dirt. Or a small hill in an otherwise flat area. No, it definitely looked like a pile of dirt. It was pretty far away though; the beam of her flashlight barely reached it. She turned and began walking toward it, moving the beam up and down and all around the form, trying to discern whether it really was what she hoped it was.

She was excited enough by the prospect of finding the object of her quest that she overlooked two things. The first thing was the fact that a flashlight beam moving over a large something would be quite visible from the road. The second thing was the open grave right in front of her.

"Oof!"

She dropped the flashlight as she plummeted into the grave and her glasses almost, but not quite, fell off. The knit cap did fall off though, and she banged her knee rather hard against the top of the wooden casket she found herself sprawled upon. She righted her glasses and fetched her flashlight, which had landed half upright against the earthen walls, shining its beam up the wall and onto the hopelessly weather-faded gravestone above. But Maggie knew it had once said Catrìona. And Maggie knew she was sitting on top what had once *been* Catrìona.

The smell wasn't as bad as the grave in Greyfriars. Maybe it had been so long that there was nothing left to smell. She suspected it might smell worse inside the coffin, but she had no intention of finding out. Even if she'd wanted to, she wasn't sure how she'd manage to open the lid while standing on it. But she didn't want to. Instead she decided to see if she could figure out from the scrapes where the grave robber had pried open the casket and cast a diving spell there. Then get the hell out of there before anyone—dead or undead—found her.

"<Hey! You there!>" came the Gaelic shout above her.

Too late. She instinctively clicked off the flashlight, like that would do any good. All it did was confirm she was down there. A moment later, a light shone down on her and she could make out the uniform of what was likely the only police officer in Ayrsduff.

"<What are you doing down there?> he demanded.

"Uh....<Help!>" Maggie decided to try.

"<Help?>"

"<Yes, help. Oh, help, help! I was out, um, jogging when I fell into this hole. It's not really a grave, is it?>"

The officer tipped back his hat and scratched his head. "<You were jogging through a graveyard at one in the morning?>" He shone the light on her again. "<Dressed all in black?>"

Maggie didn't like his tone. "<Help!>" she repeated. "<Help me out of here.>"

The officer hesitated, but he could hardly refuse. He knelt at the edge of the grave and reached down to pull her out.

"<Oh, thank you, thank you,>" Maggie panted as she scrambled out of the grave. "<I don't know what would have happened to me if you hadn't come by.>"

The officer didn't say anything for a few seconds, instead regarding her with a suspicious gaze. Finally, he asked, *"Beurla?"* The Gaelic word for 'English.'

But the last thing Maggie wanted to do was speak English. Her American accent would be unmistakable. No, it was better to have a strange, but unplaceable, accent in Gaelic, than an accent that was easily identified in English—and remembered for reporting it to Sgt. Warwick and her evil partner when they eventually tracked her movements to Ayrsduff.

"<No, thank you. I prefer Gaelic.>" Then she decided the less said the better. "<Well, I guess I better finish my run. Thanks again.>"

But the officer reached out and grabbed her shoulder. "<Wait. I need to ask you a few questions.>"

"<What sort of questions?>" Maggie asked innocently. "<I told you. I was out jogging and I fell into this hole. It's very dark tonight.>"

"<It's very dark every night in Ayrsduff.>"

She had no doubt of that. "<Well, then, they shouldn't leave these holes lying about.>"

"<You shouldn't go jogging at one in the morning in a graveyard,>" the policeman countered.

Maggie nodded exaggeratedly. "<Yes, yes. You're absolutely right. I understand that now. And I can tell you, I won't make the same mistake again.>"

She was done falling into open graves. If the third time was the charm, she didn't want to know what the charm would be.

The officer seemed off balance by Maggie's apparent denseness. She decided to press her advantage. He was very young, maybe a year or two her junior, and not entirely unattractive. She stepped closer to him. "<What did you say your name was?>" she asked.

"<Uh, I didn't say,>" he stammered. "<But it's Eamonn. Officer Eamonn MacEachran.>"

"<Well, Officer Eamonn MacEachran, I should thank you properly for saving me.>" She leaned forward and kissed his cheek. "<Thank you.>"

That did it. Young Eamonn was stunned just enough for Maggie to slip away. "<Good bye.>" And before he could gather his wits enough to argue, she disappeared into the night. This time the flashlight was directed squarely in front of her feet and she ran all the way back to the hotel.

* * *

Maggie opened the hotel's front door slowly and peered inside. It was just as dark and silent as she'd left it. Once she stepped inside and locked the door behind her, she reached down and took off her shoes. Even after the sprint from the cemetery, there was still some moist grave soil on them. She didn't need Rhona asking why muddy footprints from the front door to Maggie's room had suddenly appeared overnight. She snuck slowly up the stairs, each step creaking at least as loudly as on her way out. She hurried down the hallway, dimmed flashlight in one hand, muddy shoes in the other. When she reached her door, she awkwardly fished the key out of her pocket and finally collapsed into the safety of her room.

After her door closed again, so too did the door to another room, which Maggie had completely failed to notice was cracked open as she tip-toed past.

* * *

The next day presented Maggie with a quandary. They'd booked two nights, so she would have another chance to go grave-diving. The question was how to spend the day with Philip when all she really wanted was for the day to end. She could try one of her ditches and head to the cemetery for a daytime attempt, but she wasn't keen on trying the magic in broad daylight, and since Ayrsduff was approximately six buildings long, she doubted she could really lose Philip long enough to accomplish her goal anyway.

That meant a very long day in a very small town for a very impatient Maggie.

So she was stunned—albeit pleasantly so—when, after lunch, Philip suggested a walk through the cemetery.

"Really?" Maggie asked, as if he'd just asked her to fly to Paris with him on his private jet.

"Sure," Philip replied. "In old towns like this, the cemeteries go back for centuries. I bet there are some pretty interesting people buried in this town. Pirates, rum-runners, witches…"

"Witches?" Maggie nearly choked.

"Well, not real witches," Philip clarified. "But didn't Rhona say there was a witch whose grave was just dug up? I bet we could find that easily enough."

Easier than at night, Maggie thought. "I bet you're right."

"Let's go then." Philip stood up from their lunch table. "Let's find the dug-up grave of the Ayrsduff Witch."

"Yes." Maggie stood up as well and smiled. "Let's."

* * *

"Well, that was easy," Philip remarked as they reached the grave.

Try it at one in the morning with just a flashlight, Maggie thought.

"Catrìona NicInnes Ramsay," Philip read the weathered gravestone. "Huh. I wonder why they dug her up."

"I wonder *who* dug her up," Maggie remarked.

Philip nodded. "Good point." He peered into the grave. "I bet *she* knows."

Maggie cocked her head at him. "Who? Catrìona?"

Philip shrugged. "Well, whoever did this probably had a reason they selected her out of all the graves in this cemetery. And it's not like anyone comes to Ayrsduff on their way to somewhere else. This was very specific to her. I bet she'd know why they chose her. It's a shame we can't ask her."

Maggie turned and looked into the grave too. After a moment, she nodded. "It sure is."

* * *

Dinner was at the pub. Nothing fancy, but good food and a room filled with amiable Gaelic conversation. Maggie insisted they speak only Gaelic too. It was good practice, she reminded him. And who knew if Officer Eamonn MacEachran might stop by. As a result, however, Philip didn't talk much and it wasn't long before they headed back to the hotel.

Rhona was in the sitting room, feet up on an ottoman and reading a large book by the small fire. "<Hello, you two.>" She looked up from her book as they walked in. "<Did you have a good day in our little town?>"

"<Oh, yes.>" Maggie knew Philip wouldn't mind if she did the talking. "<A walk through the graveyard and dinner at the pub.>"

"<The graveyard?>" Rhona asked. "<Did you see poor Catrìona's grave all dug up?>"

Maggie nodded. *Twice*, she thought. Instead, she said, "<Yes. Philip said it's too bad we can't ask her why she was dug up.>"

Rhona looked to Philip then back to Maggie, a strange expression unfurling cautiously on her face. "<Actually, lass,>" she said. <"We can.>"

38. Séance

Rhona led Maggie and Philip into the hotel's drawing room. It looked more like a library, with floor-to-ceiling bookshelves, an oriental rug, and a large oak table centered under an ornate chandelier.

"What? No crystal ball?" Philip whispered to Maggie, in English even.

"Shh," she rebuked him. This was serious. She knew that, even if Philip didn't.

"<The veil between the here and the hereafter is thinner than most people realize,>" Rhona explained as she closed the doors behind them. "<Many spirits remain close, ready, even eager, for contact with our world.>"

Maggie nodded. She knew that was true.

"<Many initiate the contact,>" Rhona went on as she sat and gestured for Maggie and Philip to join her, "<but others must be called.>"

Maggie knew that was true too. She sat down next to Rhona. Philip hesitated, then sat down as well, on the other side of their host. Rhona reached out and took their hands. "<We can contact the spirit world, but we must all believe. I grew up believing, watching my grandmother and then my mother contact spirits. But they

won't come if they don't feel welcome.>"

Maggie and Rhona both looked at Philip.

"What?" he said, again in English.

"<Maybe you should wait outside,>" Maggie suggested, decidedly in Gaelic.

He looked hurt. "<No,>" he managed to reply in Gaelic, although he seemed to have trouble even with that simple reply. "<I am believing.>"

Maggie wasn't sure she was—believing him, that is. But she did want him to stay. Iain had freaked out when he'd seen too much too fast. Maybe, if this worked, it might be easier for Philip to accept other things. Things about her. If they got that far.

<All right then. Let's proceed,>" Rhona said. She turned to Maggie. "<Whom are we seeking?>"

Maggie was about to reply with the name of her Ayrsduff ancestor. That was why they were doing it in the first place. To ask the ghost of Catrìona Ramsay if she knew why, some three centuries after her death, someone had disturbed her earthly remains. But Maggie didn't just know that there were ghosts, that some stayed close, and that others could be summoned. She also knew that the ones who didn't stay close might not like to be summoned. That summoning a three-hundred-year-old spirit from the serenity of the next world was inconsiderate, arrogant, and improper. At least for something like this. Catrìona had left this plane ages ago. It was best to leave it left.

But that didn't mean Maggie didn't have an answer to Rhona's question.

"Sarah MacKenzie," she said suddenly. "<Summon the ghost of Sarah MacKenzie.>"

Philip nearly swallowed his tongue. "Sarah MacKenzie?! Are you kidding?" Again with the English, as if the question wasn't irritating enough.

Maggie met his gaze with a steely glare. "<No.>"

He stared back for a moment, then nodded. "<Okay, then.>"

Rhona stood up. She lit several candles about the room and dimmed the chandelier. Then she sat down and took their hands again.

"<Oh, spirits in the great beyond,>" she began, eyes closed and face turned up to the ceiling. Philip raised an eyebrow to Maggie, but her scowl discouraged any more disrespect. He just closed his eyes too. Maggie followed suit, and Rhona continued. "<We mortal souls come humbly before you to ask for an audience with the spirit of Sarah MacKenzie, late of this world, and now part of yours. We would ask her for knowledge unattainable in our realm.>"

Maggie cracked her eyes open and peered around the room, scanning for any sign of Sarah's ghost. Rhona opened her eyes too. Philip didn't bother. Nothing happened.

"<Oh, spirits,>" Rhona repeated, "<send us Sarah MacKenzie that we might seek her counsel.>"

Again, nothing.

Rhona frowned. Maggie did too. They both looked at Philip, who had finally opened his eyes.

"<It's not me,>" he insisted, finally in fluent Gaelic. "<I'd love to see her spirit appear.>"

Rhona closed her eyes for a few moments, then opened them again and looked to Maggie. "<She isn't answering the call.>"

Maggie frowned. "<Why not?>"

Rhona shook her head. "<I'm not sure. How did she die?>"

"<Suicide,>" Maggie answered.

Rhona nodded and let go of their hands. "<Ah. I should have asked. She left this plane of her own accord. She wanted to

leave. She won't want to come back.>"

Maggie ran her hands through her thick hair. "Damn," she muttered. She should have realized. Then Rhona told her something else she should have realized.

"<Sometimes, when it comes to gaining insight from the departed, the best we can ever do is revisit what they told us when they were still alive.>"

39. Brìghde's Journal, Interrupted

No more séances. No more graveyards. Just home. Philip couldn't drive fast enough. She needed to get home. Right then. That night. She needed to read the journal. Brìghde's journal.

She needed to understand.

She was afraid she already did.

When Philip finally pulled up to her flat late that night, Maggie jumped out of the car with barely a "Thanks" shouted over her shoulder and sprinted toward her door. Philip yelled something about leaving for the conference the next day, but she ignored him. There was nothing that would delay her from what she needed to see.

Well, almost nothing.

"Maggie?"

She turned toward the voice that had come from the dark of the nearby bushes. She knew the voice.

"Iain?"

He stepped from the shadows. "Aye. It's me." The dim light of the distant streetlights played off his chiseled features. Somehow, his blue eyes shone even in the dark.

Maggie closed her own eyes and shook her head slightly. "What are you doing here? Why aren't you in Edinburgh with

Bonnie?"

"Heather," Iain corrected quietly. "And because we need to talk."

"So you thought attacking me from the bushes in the dark of night would be a good way to talk?"

"I've been here all day, Maggie," Iain explained. "Sitting on your steps waiting for you to get home. I was just leaving when you pulled up."

He glanced toward the street. "Who was that with you?"

Maggie winced. This wasn't what she had planned right then. "That was Philip. He's just a friend."

Iain smiled. "Aye, just a friend. I know the feeling." Then he asked, "The same Philip that Ellen was going on about?"

Maggie sighed. "Yes. But it's not exactly what she made it out to be."

That added some warmth to Iain's forlorn smile. "Oh? What is it then?"

Maggie ran a hand through her thick hair. She was really, really glad to see Iain. And it was really, really a bad time. She had a hunch. And she needed to do some research. She wasn't very patient when she had a hunch and needed to do research.

"Look," she said. "I do want to talk, but, um, can this wait?" It was late. "Are you here tomorrow too?"

Iain frowned a bit. "I was planning on driving back tonight."

Maggie nodded. "Oh."

"I suppose I could stay over," Iain said. He didn't quite manage not to look toward Maggie's flat when he said it.

No, she thought, *you're not coming inside right now.*

"It's just," Maggie felt the need to explain, "I know we need to talk, but now isn't the best time."

Iain thought for a moment, then smiled. "It never really is

with you, is it? Always something else occupying your thoughts."

Maggie felt a sting from the comment. "What, you want my thoughts consumed by you?"

Iain laughed slightly. "No, I'd prefer they weren't. I'm not sure how kind those thoughts would be any more. No, I'm just saying, maybe you should share some of those thoughts."

Maggie crossed her arms. She didn't like being told what kind of thoughts she was having about him. They were pretty damn complicated thoughts, thank you very much. And he'd earned every one of them.

"Share them?" she challenged. "With who? Someone who ran away when he first saw them?"

"I didn't run away when I saw them," Iain retorted. "You never shared your thoughts. I ran away when I saw, well, what I saw." He thought for a moment. "And I didn't run away."

"No," Maggie sneered. "You walked. Big difference."

Iain crossed his arms. "This isn't what I wanted to do. This isn't why I came."

"Why did you come then?" Maggie asked, her patience growing thin. She had things to do, and this wasn't how she wanted this conversation to go either. "To hear me apologize? To beg for your forgiveness? To supplicate myself to the great and powerful Iain Grant for being so bonny well wonderful for deigning to speak to me after I dared not tell him everything about myself? Well, too bad, buddy, because I'm not apologizing. You proved you couldn't handle the truth. You're the one who should apologize for abandoning me. And beg me for another chance."

"I'm not here to beg for another chance," Iain replied stiffly.

"Well, maybe you should be," Maggie answered. "Or maybe you should just leave."

Iain didn't say anything. He rubbed the back of his neck and shuffled his feet. Finally he said, "I don't know what I want to do."

Brìghde's journal was still inside. Maggie was still outside. She didn't have time for this any more.

"Well, when you figure it out," she said, turning back to her door and pulling out her keys. "Let me know."

Then she went inside and left Iain Grant out in the cold.

40. The Truth Hurts

She'd learned a thing a two about hiding books. The best place was on a bookshelf behind another book. She tossed some dime-store legal thriller off the shelf and reached behind it, her hand wrapping around her prize. The personal diary she had discovered months earlier beneath the floor of the kirk at the Castle of Park.

She turned immediately to the entries she'd studied before her trip to Visegrád. She'd read them before with one thing in mind—finding a kidnapped child—but now she needed to read them again, with something else in mind. Something terrible.

When she did, new words jumped out at her. New phrases came to the fore. New meaning attacked her and forced her to understand.

Monday, 22 December, A.D. 1645.

It was one year ago today that Margaret was burned as a witch. The time for mourning is now past. The time for action is now here. We must ensure nothing like this ever happens again. I shall send out coded missives calling together the coven. We shall meet in two moons here at Park. We must unite to eradicate the darkness which consumed my daughter lest someone else's daughter also be consumed in flame. We carry the torch of the Shining Folk, but we must shine without burning.

+++

Thursday, 18 January, A.D. 1646.

*Margaret would have been twenty-six today. I spoke with mother. **She said the magic feels weaker somehow**. I do not feel it myself. Still, I shall be sure to raise the topic with my sisters next month.*

+++

Tuesday, 26 February, A.D. 1646.

*The meeting went well. We are united in purpose. We shall use our resources and our abilities to **battle the dark magic and strengthen the light magic**. The others reported that they felt no weakening of the light magic. **All agreed to keep watch for any signs of such weakening**.*

+++

Saturday, 29 May, A.D. 1646.

*I visited with Rhonwyn ab-Morgan today. She was in Inverness with her husband on business. She convinced him to stop at Park on their way back south. She asked how I was doing since Margaret's death. I told her what I could. **I also told her of mother's concerns. She said she thought she felt it too, but was uncertain**. She spoke of a Welsh prophecy in which **the magic eventually disappears**. She stated her belief that the disappearance of the magic was connected to the phrase 'The Celtic Continent.' It was agreed that she would return in the summer with details. I shall reconvene the coven for then.*

+++

Monday, 4 June, A.D. 1646.

I spoke with Catherine today. She suggested calling for envoys from the other Celtic lands—'our sisters abroad' she called them—

to see if they know anything of this prophecy. It was agreed, but we shall forego an envoy from Brittany just now given that the prophecy threatens to come to pass on 'The Celtic Continent.'

+++

Friday, 1 August, A.D. 1646.

*The coven was convened today. Ambassadors were also present from Wales, Cornwall, Ireland and Man. Rhonwyn brought word of the prophecy. If it is true, then **the magic shall eventually abandon the Celts**, and we shall be helpless against our enemies. It was resolved: our mission is now two-fold. **We shall contain and destroy the dark magic even as we protect and preserve the light**. As **the prophecy is not meant to come to pass until centuries hence**, a blood oath was taken. Each of us shall pass our charge, mother to daughter, as long as necessary. I shall pass mine to Margaret's daughter, Catrìona, when she is old enough to understand. The coven shall meet every seven years, or more often as is necessary to track our progress. **I can only hope the day never comes where the dark arts of blood and death have survived while the light arts of soul and healing have perished**.*

+++

Saturday, 1 August, A.D. 1647.

*I had **the most horrible dream** last night. **The light magic was gone**. And a traitor, a Judas, had wrestled control of the coven, leading them toward the well of darkness, destroying all we will have worked for generation upon generation. It happened well beyond my lifetime or even Catrìona's. And so now I am tormented by two questions: Who will this Judas be? And will my own descendant be up to the challenge of stopping her?*

Maggie set the journal open on her dining room table, then

dug through her backpack for Stuart's 'The Unabridged History of Science' book. He'd insisted she take it after their trip to Edinburgh, since she'd missed some of the exhibit "searching for the loo." The only reason she'd agreed to take it was because she knew it was a library book and she thought that maybe, if she didn't return it, Stuart would lose his library rights, or at least get a big fine.

She set it next to the journal and opened it too, comparing dates and events.

In 1646, Brìghde felt the magic weaken. Just a few years earlier, in 1642, Galileo—recanter of the truth—died and Newton—revealer of the truth—was born. What was it that plaque in the museum said?

When Newton published his Principia, *in 1687 he laid the*
groundwork for our modern science-based world.

And the groundwork for the destruction of the old, magic-based one, Maggie realized.

She swallowed hard and thumbed through the advancements that followed Newton's uncovering the most fundamental understanding of how things—all things—worked.

Scientists mastered astronomy, harnessed electricity, unleashed industry.

Scientists invented steam power, discovered diesel power, unlocked nuclear power.

Scientists built machines to travel under the waves, through the sky, to the moon.

Mystery fueled curiosity. Curiosity led to science. Science supplanted mystery.

Science replaced magic.

She recalled Stuart's words in front of that stupid sheep exhibit:

"There's something special, intangible, almost magical about life. Humankind has always longed to create life, to resurrect the dead, the beat back the natural and inescapable cycle of life and death, whether it was Mary Shelly or the Scottish scientists who cloned Dolly. The dream has always been the same, to unlock the greatest scientific mystery ever: life. And this is exactly when they did it."

The year the white magic finally died, fully supplanted by the cold logic of science. There was no further need for white magic to short-cut the rules of physics; the rules of physics could take care of themselves just fine now, thank you. If you wanted to fly, you didn't need a levitation spell; just build a spaceship. If you wanted to see something on the other side of the world, you didn't need a divining spell; just look at the satellite images. If you wanted to unleash the power of a million fires, no need to delve into arcane arts; just take the simplest thing in the universe, a Hydrogen atom, and crack it open.

The white magic died and, within a year, so did her mother. Heart failure, they said. Now Maggie knew better. Or rather, now she knew why. And her own heart broke.

She slumped to the floor and tried to deny the undeniable. She considered the rush she always got when she used the dark magic, totally worth the ensuing nightmares. What must it have been like to wield the white magic? Just as powerful, but positive, with no ill effects? Rather than nightmares of Hell, did you dream of Heaven? What must it have been like to feel that magic ebbing? And what must it have been like to have been the last one to know the magic, weak as it was, and then feel it disappear forever?

It must have been unbearable.

She turned and spotted the photo frame across the room. She raised her hand and unleashed the levitation spell. The frame flew across the room and smacked into her outstretched hand. She glared at the image with welling tears. It was her as a child, standing beside her mother and her grandmother. Before her mother died. Before her mother abandoned her, a child of only eight. And for the first time ever, she looked at the photo understanding why her mother had left. She finally understood.

But she didn't have to forgive.

She'd fought her whole life against the hate she wanted to feel at her mother for not staying alive. She could win that battle when the reason she died was something out of her mother's control. When it was just that something happened, something medical, something unavoidable.

But now Maggie knew it wasn't medical. It wasn't unavoidable. It didn't just happen. Her mother lost the magic and she gave up. On everything. On Maggie.

And Maggie finally released the hate.

The frame shot across the room and smashed against the wall. The photo inside burst into flames. She carefully picked up Brìghde's journal and cradled it in her arms. Then she lowered her head and unleashed her fury.

Books flew off her bookshelves. Frames crashed against the wall. Light bulbs exploded. She curled into a ball and sobbed as of all her books and belongings and treasures and memories flew over her head to break and burn and die.

41. Destined to Fail

She passed out. She must have. When she woke up, she was laying in the middle of her flat, debris everywhere, her head throbbing and her heart racing, and Brìghde's journal still clutched in her hands.

But first, before she woke up, she dreamt…

It was raining. Not a downpour, but more than a drizzle. And the rain was cold. The drops pierced her linen sleeves and drove into her skin like needles. The ground remained parched though. The raindrops sizzled and popped into steam as they hit the cracked earth, filing the air with an ear-splitting buzz and a foul-smelling mist as Maggie marched across the broken plain toward the stone fortress at its center.

She didn't have much time. The gray clouds above her were melding into a darker, almost black ring of clouds which was closing in over her head. The storm was coming. She needed to get to the keep before it was too late. Before everything was lost, forever.

She could feel their eyes on her as she strode toward the castle. They didn't attack her this time. They just watched, either afraid to engage her or, more likely, aware they needn't bother. This was the endgame. She knew it. They knew it. She would be allowed into the castle. They had no intention of letting her out again.

The demons flitted invisible in her peripheral vision, disappearing into the ether when she turned to look at them directly. She couldn't tell how many there were, except to know there were too many.

She lowered her shoulders and marched on.

The castle loomed at the center of the parched plain. When she reached the structure, she looked up at the iron drawbridge. It was up. But she knew it would drop for her.

A clap of thunder echoed across the darkening sky.

Then she heard a loud clank and the drawbridge started to descend, its heavy chains rattling as the entrance lowered itself directly toward her.

The rain grew heavier. The demons danced in the corners of her eyes. The ground crackled with steam and fire. And the drawbridge slammed to the ground right in front of her feet.

A dare.

She stepped onto the bridge and walked across it and into the castle.

She knew the demons followed behind. And more awaited within.

Inside the castle, the ground was lush. A thick blanket of emerald grass stretched over the entire courtyard, and a tall, twisted tree rose from the center of the yard, its tangled branches reaching toward the last spot of gray being swallowed by the black clouds swirling above.

Maggie walked directly to the tree. As she approached, thirteen huge, crooked rocks pushed up through the grass, forming a stone circle around the tree—and her. She stopped. The ground directly between her and the tree opened up, spilling down into itself to create a perfectly rectangular hole at her feet.

A grave.

Her grave.

Or so they intended.

She stepped around the grave and reached the tree. That's when the demons revealed themselves. A mob of demons, dozens deep, surrounded the stone circle, pressing against the cairns, but not entering. They weren't there to attack her. They were there to prevent her escape.

The sky was completely black now. The rain drove down in torrents, freezing her clothes and skin. From within twelve of the thirteen stones stepped a beautiful young woman, each dressed in a different style of the same cream-colored linen dress. The rain didn't seem to hit them. They remained dry and glowing and beautiful. They all raised their hands and stepped toward her.

"Maggie," they said in unison, their voices bypassing her ears to echo directly inside her mind.

She raised her own hands—into a fighting stance, and glared at the illusions.

They stopped. Then they disappeared.

The background chattering of the demons rose into a high-pitched screech. The earth shifted beneath her feet. The cairns—and the ground within their circle—began to spin, like a calliope, with the stones as the horses and the demons as the crowd of onlookers waiting for the next ride. The spinning accelerated—faster and faster. The tree's branches sliced through the air as it orbited the grave at the very center of the circle. The rotation distorted the grave from a clean rectangle to a gaping oval, a mouth opening to swallow Maggie. The stones began to rise at the edges, but the grave remained low and at the center, turning the calliope into a funnel. Maggie began sliding toward the grave, slipping on the grass despite her best efforts to stand her ground.

The spinning went even faster. The stones rose even higher. Maggie slipped even more relentlessly toward the grave. Her grave. She dropped to the angled ground and dug her heels into the thick grass.

She stopped herself just short of the opening, her heels and fingertips deep in the grass, keeping her—just barely—out of the abyss.

Then the spinning suddenly stopped. The earth was flat again. The grave was rectangular again. The tree branches rustled as they skittered to a halt. The rain stopped. Even the demon-screech went silent.

She exhaled and relaxed her grip on the grass.

Then twelve pairs of glowing hands reached up from the grave and pulled her in.

She screamed as they pushed her to the bottom of the grave. The cold mud squelched up around her neck and back and limbs. The women weren't beautiful anymore. They weren't spirits; they were zombies again. Dead and rotten and decaying—strong as iron and stinking of death.

She tried to use the magic to push them off of her, but it didn't work. The magic fizzled and failed, like the raindrops on the burning plain. The magic was gone. She was helpless.

Then the roots came.

Roots from the tree snaked out of the earthen walls. Dozens of them. They undulated toward her like snakes, worms. But rather than wrap around her wrists like she might have expected, the tips of the roots rested on her skin—at her hands and feet, arms and legs, stomach and shoulders. Then they drove into, and through, her flesh, pinning her body into the grave.

She screamed as the roots continued to extend, snaking

through her limbs and torso, fixing her to the spot and spilling her blood and guts into the earth.

"Why don't you heal yourself?" a voice taunted from above.

The zombies were gone, their duties completed by the roots.

"Heal yourself, healer," came another taunt.

The same voice. Maggie recognized it.

She looked up. The sky was black. She looked to the side. The grave was black. She looked down. The blood oozed black from her body. A new root wound its way over to her and pressed its tip against her forehead.

"You can't heal yourself, can you, healer?"

Maggie struggled to answer against the pain consuming her body. She couldn't see the face peering down at her. She could never see the goddamned face. But she knew the voice.

"No, mama," she answered. "I can't."

Then the root drove itself through her skull and everything went dark.

It was finally over. She'd failed.

42. Half-Baked Explanations

Maggie woke after the nightmare, but couldn't find the energy to get up. Instead, she passed out again, hopeful that the single dream had been sufficient penance for using the magic. When she woke next it was to a pounding on her door and the sound of another familiar voice: Ellen's.

"Maggie! Maggie! Are you in there? Are you okay? Open up!"

Maggie forced herself into a sitting position and looked around. The place was trashed. Books and baubles littered the floor and furniture. Shards of broken glass and wisps of burnt paper mixed with fallen pictures and thrown-open books. She looked down and saw that she was still holding Brìghde's journal.

Knock! Knock! Knock! "Maggie?!"

She put a hand on her coffee table and pushed herself to her feet. "Hold on," she croaked. "I'm coming."

Her head was throbbing and her whole body ached. But worse was the sharp pain she felt in her hands and feet, legs and arms, stomach and shoulders. And especially her forehead. All the places where the roots had pierced her body. It was as if they were still there, impaling her to the bottom of the grave. She shuffled painfully across the floor and unlocked the door.

"Maggie?!"

Ellen was aghast, and it occurred to Maggie that she might look almost as bad as she felt. Maybe she should have checked the mirror before opening the door. And in case it wasn't mortifying enough looking like hell in front of her friend, Ellen had brought along Stuart and some other guy Maggie had never seen but whose identity she was vaguely aware she ought to be able to deduce. But forget that. Her brain was busy trying to convince her stomach not to vomit.

She didn't say anything to her guests. Instead, she turned and walked back into her apartment. She shoved just enough stuff out of the way to be able to sit on her couch. She didn't try to clear space for the others.

Ellen and Stuart stepped in, but remained standing, mouths agape at the carnage. The other guy had no trouble following Maggie's example, though. He not only cleared off a chair, but slid half the crap off of the coffee table so he could set down a laptop. *Her* laptop. He turned it on and cracked his knuckles.

Ah, she thought. *Computer guy.* She didn't bother trying to remember his name. The label was adequate.

Ellen's head surveyed the wreckage like it was on a swivel. "What happened, Mags?"

Maggie looked around too. "Tornado," she said. "Or earthquake. I haven't decided yet."

"We don't have tornadoes here," Ellen replied.

"Then earthquake," Maggie said. "Definitely earthquake."

"We don't have those either."

"Oh really?" Maggie waved at the carnage. "Then how do you explain all this?"

Ellen just shook her head. "There's no talking to you sometimes."

Maggie decided to change the subject. "Why are you here?"

"Philip called me," Ellen answered. "He was worried about you."

"Aw." Maggie smiled. "That's nice.

"And we made some progress on your computer," said Computer Guy. "I'm Dougie," he reminded her.

"Ah." Maggie nodded. More good news. Philip, worried. Computer, progress. Now if she could just get that tree root out of her brain... "What did you find out?"

"Well, I haven't finished yet," Dougie said, his fingers dashing across the keyboard. "I still don't know exactly who is sending you those emails, but I did find something very interesting about them."

Maggie wondered whether it was really all that interesting, or just interesting to a computer nerd. But it turned out to be interesting to a Gaelic studies nerd too.

Dougie turned the laptop so Maggie could see the screen as well. "Okay," he said. "I've managed to access the sender's account. The first thing that's interesting is that there are no other email contacts except for you. The second thing is that it was opened just before the first email was sent to you."

During The Lost Weeks. Maggie nodded.

"But the really interesting part," Dougie went on, "is that all of the emails were drafted at the same time and then queued for later delivery."

Maggie frowned. "What does that mean?"

"It means," Dougie explained, "that whoever is sending you these emails is doing it on auto-pilot. They sat down, weeks ago, and wrote all of the emails at once. Then they scheduled them to be sent out, one at a time, in a very specific order, at very specific dates and times."

Maggie wasn't sure what to make of the information. Was it good or bad? It meant someone was trying to trick her, which was never good. On the other hand, it appeared no one was actually stalking her every move.

"Why would they do that?" she asked.

"Why?" Dougie repeated with a shrug. "I dunno. That's human stuff. I'm computers. I can tell you what someone's doing on, but I can't say why."

Maggie thought for a moment. Whoever it was must have known she would come looking for them. "Is it so they can just delete them all at once and erase their tracks?"

"Well, first of all," Dougie raised a finger, "you can't ever completely erase your tracks. Everything is stored somewhere. Even when you delete something on your laptop, it's still there."

Maggie grimaced. "Like my browsing history?"

Dougie nodded and grinned. "Exactly."

Maggie shook her head. Which hurt. So she stopped. Damned root…

"Deleting something doesn't actually get rid of it," Dougie went on. "It just makes those bytes available for new data to be written over it. But if the computer never puts anything over those bytes, all that supposedly deleted data is still there. And that's even more true for things online, like email. Everything important is still there, invisible, but just waiting to get pulled out again."

"Oh." Maggie found herself disappointed to hear that. She kind of liked to hide stuff. She certainly didn't want someone to see all the things she'd tried to keep secret.

"But here's the really exciting part." Dougie tapped the screen.

Maggie noticed they'd graduated from interesting to exciting. She leaned forward and tried to focus on the screen.

"These," said Dougie pointing a folder labeled 'SENT', "are the emails that have already been sent."

Maggie nodded. She knew how to use email.

But then Dougie tapped another folder, labeled 'DRAFTS.' "And these are the ones that have been written, but haven't been sent yet. There are two left."

Maggie's eyes widened. Okay, yes. That was exciting. "Can we read them now? Before they're sent?"

"Yep." Dougie smiled. "In fact, one's scheduled for tomorrow, Halloween."

"Samhain," Maggie corrected.

"Uh, sure. If you say so," Dougie replied uncertainly. But Maggie knew that was the important holiday. "And the other is scheduled for the next day, November first."

Maggie's eyes were glued to the screen. "Open them up. The one for tomorrow first."

Dougie nodded. He clicked a couple of times and the email filled the screen. Maggie leaned forward and read it aloud.

"Date: October 31. Subject: Last Chance. I'm watching you. You must stay home tonight. Bolt your door. Let no one in. Await further instructions."

"Well, that's certainly friendly," Ellen remarked.

"And a lie," Dougie pointed out. "Whoever wrote this, wrote it weeks ago. They're not watching you."

Maggie nodded, understanding Dougie's point, but not completely convinced. Just because it had been weeks since the sender said he'd be watching her didn't mean he didn't keep his appointment to do so. "Open the next one."

Dougie nodded and clicked. Maggie read.

"Date: November 1. Subject: The Book. Well done. You have passed all my tests. The Dark Book can be yours again. You will find it where you found the diary, and you will know who I am and why I did this."

Maggie's heart began pounding in her chest. The Book. Her Book. She was finally going to get the Dark Book back.

"There's that Dark Book again," Ellen said. "And what diary?"

Maggie forced herself not to look down. Brìghde's diary was still in her hand.

Ellen grinned. "You're not going to tell me, are you?"

Maggie hesitated, then shook her head ever so slightly.

"Are you staying in tomorrow night?" Ellen followed up. She looked to Stuart and Dougie. "Do you want us to stay with you?"

"I'm not staying in," Maggie replied, her eyes still on the computer screen.

"Are you going to the conference at Callanish with Philip?" Ellen tried.

"No."

"Are you going to tell me?" Ellen pressed.

Maggie finally looked up at her friend. She smiled. "No."

Ellen sighed and shook her head. But she was smiling too. "Do you need a ride?"

Maggie hesitated. She needed a way to get there, but she needed privacy too.

Ellen reached into her purse and pulled out a set of keys. "How about a car?"

Maggie didn't know what to say. "Thanks, Ellen."

"Sure thing," Ellen answered. She handed Maggie the keys. "Tell me afterward, okay? Some day, when it's all over, tell me."

Maggie wrapped her hand around the keys and nodded. "I promise."

43. Recovered and Discovered

Maggie wasted no time. Before she could do much more than grab her laptop and kick out her friends, she was on the road. She was halfway to her destination before she realized the message light was flashing on her phone. She figured it was Philip, calling about the conference. Nope.

Beep! "Um, hi, Maggie. This is, uh, Iain. Iain Grant. Aye, well, you probably knew that part. Well, anyway, uh, I don't really like leaving messages. I tend to ramble on a bit. I guess I'm doing that right now. So, uh, I'll just get right to the point. I'm still in Aberdeen. And, um I was just wondering if, maybe, if you wanted to, well, maybe we could try to talk again. Um, all right then, I guess that's it. So, aye, ring me up if you're interested. 'Bye."

She pressed the phone against her head as she sped down the motorway and sighed. What she wouldn't give to talk to Iain. To straighten things out. To listen and have him listen. To be riding next to him right then. But she had to get her Book. Now that she finally knew where it was, she had to get it. And she knew he wouldn't understand. Damn him.

She pulled the phone away from her face, hesitated for a moment, then pressed '7'. *"Your message has been deleted."*

* * *

The Castle of Park was actually a noble residence built as a home for the chieftains of the Clan Innes—Maggie's clan. Maggie had first visited it the previous fall with her aunt and uncle, exploring the grounds and staying at the part of the castle which had been converted to a hotel. It was on that trip that she had discovered both the portrait and the grave of her ancestor, Brìghde Innes—the Healer. The grave was in the small kirkyard which surrounded the now-deconsecrated private kirk the Inneses used as their personal church. Also on the grounds, but just outside the iron fence around the kirkyard, was another grave. The grave of Brìghde's daughter, Margaret NicInnes Wilkie—the Witch.

Her second visit was with Iain (*sigh*) and it was on that visit that, guided by a dream rather than an email, that Maggie had discovered Brìghde Innes' private journal, hidden for centuries beneath a loose floorstone in the kirk.

Now Maggie had returned for a third visit. Her goals were many. Primarily, she had come to fetch her Dark Book from the same secret vault from which she'd extracted Brìghde's diary. But in addition, she had come to guard Brìghde's and Margaret's graves. Samhain was the next day. Catrìona's grave had already been hit. That left two graves: Brìghde's and Margaret's. She'd been too late for Catrìona, but she'd get to Park just in time. She hoped.

But as she drove Ellen's car up the long drive to the castle-cum-hotel, the police car in the parking lot told her was she was too late again.

She stepped into the lobby just as the officers were getting ready to leave.

"Thank you for your help," one of them was saying to the front desk woman.

"The inspector will be around tomorrow," said the other, "if she has any follow-up questions."

"All right then," answered the woman. She was young—likely a local girl who'd scored a job at the tourist hotel—with straight black hair and a sharp white blouse.

"Good day, miss," said the first police officer as they stepped around Maggie and out to their car.

The receptionist echoed the cops. "Good day, miss." Then, "Can I help you?"

Maggie watched after the departing police officers, then turned back. "Uh, yes. I called on my way here. I have a reservation for tonight. The name is Maggie Devereaux."

The receptionist typed a few entries into her computer. "Ah, yes. We've only one other guest right now so I gave you our best room: the Black Watch Suite. Have you stayed with us before?"

The Black Watch Suite was the room she'd shared with Iain. She sighed. "Yes," she answered. "A couple of times actually."

"Oh, wonderful," the young woman replied. "Well, then, you know you're free to follow the walking trails across the grounds. The only exception is on account of those police officers you just saw. We had a bit of mischief last night in the cemetery by the old kirk, so that area is off-limits for the time being, I'm afraid. You'll see the police tape, so just stay on this side of it and you'll be fine."

Maggie nodded. She expected that was true, even if she had no intention of staying on this side of it. She finished checking in and dropped her one bag in her room. Then she went for a walk. It was still early afternoon and if she hadn't been sure whether she would wait until the cover of darkness to break into the kirk (again), the presence of the police had helped settle it. All she could do was kill time and wait for nightfall.

It was a long, thoughtful walk. There were miles of trails across the estate. She saw the orchard, the ponds, both waterfalls, and the rhododendron tunnel. She also saw the small, boarded-up church she'd be visiting that night, and the blue-and-white police tape in the adjoining graveyard. And when she got back to the castle, she saw a new rental car in the lot. Her heart raced for a moment, thinking Iain had somehow tracked her down—perhaps remembering their night in the Black Watch Suite—and come to find her to declare his love and embrace her for who she truly was.

Then she realized he had his own car and didn't need a rental. The only rental she'd ridden in was Philip's. And, she realized as she stepped into the lobby, it was Philip who had tracked her down.

"Maggie!" he jumped up from his seat in one of the lobby's wingback chairs.

It was then that she realized that Philip was actually a rather poor substitute for Iain. Iain had been a good sport—well, until the end—but he'd also given Maggie her space. Ayrsduff had been difficult enough. The last thing she needed right then was a pair of eyes watching her. What the hell was he doing there?

"Philip?" she responded in what she tried to make sound like a pleasantly surprised tone. "What are you doing here?"

"Ellen told me everything," he said, his brow creased with worry. "The emails, your ransacked apartment, everything. I came to see if you were all right."

Maggie crossed her arms and fought off a frown. Ellen shouldn't have ratted her out like that. She wasn't the squealing type, but she was the talking type. No doubt he'd asked a simple question and Ellen had spilled the whole story. Still, there was something that bothered her about Philip's explanation, but she couldn't quite put her finger on it. "I'm all right," she assured. "What about your conference?"

"Oh, who cares," he replied. "I'm sure I'll get to the cairns sooner or later. The important thing is you. I came to protect you."

Ah, that must be what bothered her. She narrowed her eyes and glared at him. "I'm not some damsel in distress. I don't need to be rescued."

Philip blanched at the reproach. "N-No, of course not," he stammered. "That didn't come out right. What I meant was, I was worried and I wanted to see if I could help."

Maggie's frown relaxed a bit. After a moment, she uncrossed her arms. *Damn it.* She was just getting used to working alone. "Okay. Well, there is one thing I can think of that I need help with."

Philip stood up straight and offered a facetious salute. "Yes, ma'am. Your wish is my command."

Maggie shook her head and wished he weren't so cute when he was being stupid. "Dinner," she said. "I hate eating alone. Will you join me?"

Philip lowered his salute and smiled. "Well, of course. Worth the drive here alone."

Maggie smiled back. She might as well enjoy dinner. She'd snuck out of the hotel in Ayrsduff without him seeing her. She was sure could do it just as well again.

* * *

Dinner was nice enough, although it did drag a little as Maggie pretended not to be wishing it away. The after-dinner chat in the lobby was a bit less bearable. Dusk was settling down invitingly. When Philip suggested a walk under the stars that were blinking into the sky to taunt her, it was too much.

"I-I'm sorry, Philip," she said. "I'm not feeling all that great. I think I better just go to bed."

"Oh," said Philip simply, but obviously crestfallen. "Okay. Sure. Uh, I hope you feel better. Should we meet for breakfast tomorrow?"

Maggie offered a friendly smile. "Of course. Tomorrow sounds perfect. I'm very much looking forward to tomorrow."

Philip returned the smile. "Me too then."

And Maggie hurried to her suite to await the night.

* * *

She knew she had to wait for more than just the onset of darkness. Before Philip arrived, when she still had some anonymity, it might have done to go out around ten o'clock, but with her Canadian suitor in the next room, she needed to wait until midnight.

Just as well, she thought. If she was going to break into a deconsecrated church to reclaim a lost book of dark magic—and she was—she couldn't think of a better hour to do it.

She set the alarm on her cell phone and allowed herself a cat nap. At 11:50, her phone beeped and she swung her feet onto the floor. It was time to go. Phone into pocket, flashlight into hand, and Maggie into hallway. A minute later she was outside, comfortable no one had seen her. She didn't hear the other door creak as she went by.

She hurried across the wet grass directly to the kirk. She was curious about the graves, but she would feel much better inspecting them after she had her Dark Book in her hands again. The front door of the kirk had been resealed with new wooden planks—a repair since her last burglary. But, even without the Book, she could enter just as easily as she had then. Combining muscle and magic, she quickly removed the boards and slipped inside, not even bothering to close the door behind her. It didn't matter. The Book was only yards away.

There was almost no light. The moon either hadn't risen yet or was too dim to help. Faint stars were visible through the gaps in the boards covering the stone-framed window above the floorstone that rested over the Dark Book.

Again the levitation spell. She knew it meant another nightmare, but she didn't care. She'd gladly suffer a night of bad dreams to wake up next to her Book in the morning. Ever since she'd lost it, its disappearance had lurked in the back of her mind, interfering with more immediate thoughts, clouding her judgment, impairing her ability to see connections and deduce answers. She was sure that once the Book was in her hands again, she would see clearly what had been going on all around her.

The heavy stone rose easily, the magic fueled by Maggie's anticipation, and she guided it to one side with a wave of her hand. She dropped to her knees and reached into the gap recklessly, just like that day in the Ancient Book Collection. And just like that day in the library, her hand felt the worn leather of the Dark Book of Rights and Damnation. *Her* Book of Rites and Damnation.

She carefully extracted the ancient tome from its hiding spot. She clutched it to her chest and choked back a sob.

"Finally."

And her mind finally calmed down enough to realize what had bothered her about Philip's explanation of how he'd known she was at Park.

She never told Ellen she was going to Park.

Then her phone chirped, a deafening beep in the silence of the ancient church. She shoved a scrambling hand in to her pocket and yanked out her phone.

There was a text. From Ellen.

Dougie traced the emails. They came from YOUR laptop. You sent them to yourself.

Maggie frowned at the text, not understanding. But she didn't have time to figure it out. The blow to the back of her head knocked her quite unconscious.

44. Last Rite

Her name was Maggie Devereaux.

She had the second worst headache of her life.

And something smelled terrible.

Last time, the smell—she'd soon learned—was the smell of recent death. This smell—she'd since learned—was the smell of old death. Decay. The grave.

In part because of the pain in her head, and in part because she was afraid of what she might see, Maggie delayed opening her eyes while she assessed her situation as best she could.

Her hands were bound behind her back. Her ankles were bound too. She was outside, the air cool, the grass damp, and the ground bumpy. She was, she knew, not alone.

She opened her eyes.

She found herself inside a circle of standing stones. She recognized them. They were the ones from her last nightmare. And now she knew they were the ones at Callanish too. She'd been transported there somehow, likely in the boot of someone's car. But, as troubling as the circumstances were, they could have been worse.

"At least I'm not in a grave," she whispered to herself.

"Not yet," came a cold reply.

Maggie recognized the voice. Just like in her dream. But it

wasn't her mother. She looked over at the woman standing at the center of the stone circle—the tomb. "Sarah MacKenzie."

"Oh, Maggie," Sarah folded her hands melodramatically across her chest, "you remembered me. It's so nice to be remembered after you've passed away."

"You're not dead," Maggie observed.

Sarah laughed. She was definitely not dead. Indeed, she looked quite lively, animated even, as she stood over an open casket, surrounded by the circle's thirteen interior stones. She was smiling ear to ear, her hair blowing in the breeze, and Maggie's Dark Book in her hands.

"No, I'm afraid not," she replied. "That was a necessary ruse. I needed cover for what I had planned. And for what I did to Derek unplanned. It was easy enough to find a transient about my age and size. It was also relatively easy to strangle her to death with a length of rope. The hard part was hoisting her over the door. And waiting two days to call the police. I thought a little extra decomposition might discourage too aggressive of attempts at identifying the body."

She grinned at the memory, obviously pleased with her own cleverness.

"But don't worry." She went on, gesturing grandly toward the box at her feet. "We've got plenty of dead people in here." She frowned into the coffin, then looked back at Maggie with a dark grin. "Well, parts of them anyway."

Maggie winced.

"Oh, it's okay," Sarah assured as she stepped back over to where Maggie lay helpless, "you get used to the smell. Well, I did anyway. I've even come to like it, because I know what it means."

Maggie felt her head clearing. She subtly tested the bonds on her hands. They were tight. *Maybe the burning spell*, she thought. It would hurt, but likely not nearly as much as whatever Sarah had planned. *Keep her talking.* "What does it mean?"

"It means the white magic is coming back, Maggie." Sarah turned again, pacing between her live and her dead victims. "Isn't that wonderful? And it's all thanks to you and your ancestors. And your book."

"Oh, well, great," Maggie replied. "You're welcome. Glad to have helped. Can I go now?"

Sarah laughed. A long, disturbing laugh. "Oh, no. You're the key to this entire endeavor, dear Maggie. You're not going anywhere."

Maggie nodded weakly. "I figured." She pulled again at her wrists, but the rope didn't budge. She wondered if she could burn the ropes at her wrists and ankles at the same time. No use having her hands free if she couldn't stand up. Well, less use anyway.

"I realized my mistake at Visegrád," Sarah went on. She stopped at the coffin and leaned onto its edges, as if examining her reflection in some unseen fountain. "I thought the magic was still here. In the air. Just waiting to be tapped into. But it's gone, isn't it, Maggie? It's gone. But not forever. Nothing is forever. They're about to clone mammoths from frozen bones. And I realized that's where the magic is too. In the bones of those who used it."

"My ancestors," Maggie realized.

"Exactly," Sarah answered. "I can do research too, my little student. It didn't take long to find the graves of everyone from you back to your glorious Healer ancestor. The magic is in their bones, and now their bones are together again."

But then Sarah frowned and her brow creased deeply. "Well, not everyone. We're missing two."

Maggie breathed a sigh of relief. Her mother and grandmother hadn't been disturbed after all.

"I didn't get the most recent bones I needed," Sarah admitted with a scowl. "I had that planned out too, but I trusted a man to do it, and if there's one thing I've learned over the years, it's never to trust a man."

Maggie didn't really care about Sarah's romantic history. But she was curious what had happened to spare her most immediate relatives from the unseemly fate of her older forebears. Plus it gave her time to remember the burning spell and consider how to administer it as maybe just a smoldering-and-weakening-the-rope spell. "What happened?"

"I discovered a Canadian professor on his way to Aberdeen," Sarah explained. "He was from Vancouver, not far from where your mother and grandmother are buried. I would have preferred someone even closer, but fortune grants wishes in her own ways. It was simple enough to friend him online and then start sending suggestive messages until he thought he'd arrive in the Highlands with a Scottish girlfriend ready to service his every desire. He had quite the interest in the occult—or so he claimed— but when he got here he didn't bring the bones I told him to bring. He said he'd do it, but he didn't. I told him exactly what to do, exactly where to go and what to get. I needed to start with a backbone. Your mother's backbone. Something sturdy upon which to build the frame of a new white magic wielder. But he failed me. He said he thought I was joking. I wasn't joking. And I showed him I wasn't joking."

"So you killed him?" Maggie asked, certain now that she would be lucky to escape with only burnt wrists and ankles.

"Well, I admit I lost my temper," Sarah said. "I gave him a chance to redeem himself. If we couldn't use your mother or grandmother as the base, maybe we could use you. We found you in Edinburgh, hooking up with that awful Sinclair man, and we came up with a plan."

Hooking up with Sinclair? Maggie thought. *Eww.* Sarah had that part wrong. Maggie didn't remember what happened during The Lost Weeks, but she was pretty sure she wouldn't have hooked up with Sinclair. On the other hand, she did wake up in his hotel room....

"What was the plan?" Maggie propped herself up into a sitting position. She hoped Sarah wouldn't notice as she continued to rant.

"To murder you and take your spine, of course," Sarah turned to tell Maggie, very matter-of-factly. She didn't seem to care about Maggie's altered position. "But that stupid Derek couldn't do that right either. You were late. He said he couldn't do it. And quite frankly, I'd lost my patience with him."

"Of course," Maggie replied. She said the burning spell inside her mind, hoping she was doing it just slightly enough to damage the ropes without searing her flesh. After a moment she thought she felt some heat at her wrists.

"I didn't kill him," Sarah thrust a finger at Maggie. "Not on purpose. I did punch him though as we waited for you in the bathroom. I guess he wasn't expecting it. He fell straight back and into the bathtub. He hit his head on the spout. It cracked his skull wide open. It sounded like a watermelon hitting the sidewalk after being thrown of a roof. It was a sign. Since he hadn't brought the bones I needed, I'd just take his."

"Makes perfect sense," Maggie assured, her wrists growing uncomfortably warm.

"Don't patronize me," Sarah snapped. Then she looked back into the casket and frowned. "I'm afraid it may compromise the spell, actually. His spine doesn't have the magic in it. So I'll need to make up for that."

Maggie didn't like the sound of that. She suspected she was somehow going to be the remedy. "So what's the plan then?" She looked around. The sky was beginning to lighten beyond the stones. "A spell at sunrise on Samhain? Kind of clichéd, don't you think?"

Sarah narrowed her eyes at her captive. "Still sassy, eh, Maggie? Well, yes, as a matter of fact. A resurrection spell. But instead of resurrecting one person, I'm going to resurrect the power of a dozen people."

"Well, ten anyway," Maggie corrected, subtracting her mother and grandmother.

Sarah frowned for a moment, then grinned at her. "Eleven."

Ugh. Maggie knew she was the eleventh. No need to ask more about that. The ropes were loosening. *Keep her talking.* "How are you going to get the white magic from the bones?"

Sarah held Maggie's Dark Book aloft. "With the dark magic!"

"But you don't know how to use the dark magic," Maggie protested.

"No," Sarah lowered the book and smiled at Maggie, "but you do."

Maggie shook her head. "I won't help you."

Sarah's grin widened. She reached into her jacket pocket and extracted a rather large handgun. "I think you will."

Maggie was startled enough that she lost her concentration on the burning spell. The ropes were weakened, but still bound her. "You're going to shoot me?!"

"Of course," Sarah replied calmly. "I need your bones too. You're going to complete my Frankenstein's monster." She reached into the casket and extracted a hacksaw. "It needs a head."

Maggie felt the adrenaline dump into her system. "Y-You're crazy if you think I'm just going to let you cut my head off." *You're crazy anyway, lady.*

"Well, you'll be dead already," Sarah explained. "I'm going to shoot you through the heart first. But not before you tell me how to use this book."

Maggie shook her head defiantly. "I'll never tell you."

Sarah smiled sweetly, almost like a mother. "Of course you will," she said.

Then she shot Maggie in the foot.

Maggie screamed as the bullet shattered her bones and sent blood pouring from the wound.

"What's the matter?" Sarah laughed. "Can't heal yourself?"

Maggie just glared up at her tormenter, blinking back tears against the pain of the gunshot wound and the echo of her dreams.

"Guess you better help me get the white magic back," Sarah said.

Maggie bit her lip against the pain, but couldn't say anything.

"Now," Sarah moved the pistol slightly so she was now aiming at Maggie's shin. "How does it work?"

When Maggie didn't immediately reply, Sarah shook the gun slightly. "You'd better tell me, Maggie. I've got five more rounds in the magazine and no one knows you're here."

"Wrong!"

Maggie and Sarah both turned to see four figures climb the hill and enter the stone circle. Ellen. Stuart. Dougie. And Iain.

"Iain!" Maggie cried. A tsunami of emotions nearly overwhelmed her. Relief. Joy. Surprise. Worry. Fear.

He strode purposefully ahead and stood between Maggie and Sarah MacKenzie's gun. "This ends now," he declared.

"Oh, good Lord," Sarah sighed and rolled her eyes. Then she shot Iain in the stomach.

"Iain!" Maggie shouted again. With barely a thought, the ropes binding her burst to flame and dropped to the ground as so much ash, blistering her wrists and ankles. She ignored her own wounds and crawled over to Iain, who lay curled up on his side, holding his stomach and moaning.

"Maybe I—*cough, cough*—shouldn't have come back for you—*cough*—after all," he joked through the pain.

"Ah, the boyfriend," Sarah said slowly. "Maybe if I make *him* suffer..."

Maggie glared up at her former professor. Maggie could feel the panic gripping her heart. But she could still control it. Barely.

Sarah flashed the gun at Ellen, Stuart, and Dougie. "You'd better run," she warned. Stuart and Dougie didn't need to be told twice. They sprinted down the hill. Ellen didn't. She retreated, but only as far as the nearest stone, crouching behind it for protection. Sarah turned back to the two in front of her.

"He's dying, Maggie," she said. "And there's no healing spell—*unless* you tell me how to use the dark magic."

Maggie hesitated. She laid a hand on Iain's shoulder. His breathing was labored. "Don't do it, Maggie," he wheezed.

"Hush!" Sarah commanded. She shot him again, this time in the leg. Blood spurted from the artery.

"Time's up, Maggie," she said. "Make a decision. I promise. I *promise* I'll heal him after I get the white magic back. The white magic is still there, Maggie. It's just waiting to be pulled out again."

Maggie looked around wildly. The coffin, the hill, the stones. The stones.

And she realized Sarah was telling the truth. Not about Iain—she'd never heal him. But about the magic. She just needed a moment to think clearly. She had to stall somehow, but Sarah was right: time was up. She looked back up at Sarah and realized she wouldn't need to stall after all.

Philip was standing right behind Sarah. He had walked up behind her during the commotion and gunshots. He raised the shovel in hands and smashed Sarah over the head.

She collapsed to the ground. The gun bounced from her limp hand. Philip picked it up and held it away from his body, like a dead rat. "I followed Sarah's car when I saw her load you into the trunk and speed out of the lot. She beat me to the ferry dock and I had to wait for the next one. I called Ellen on the way. Maggie, I don't understand what this is all about, but whatever it is— whatever you do, do it."

Maggie nodded and looked down at Iain. He managed a smile. "I'm sorry, Maggie. I'm sorry I ran away. I was scared. By you. By—*cough*—by how I felt about you. But I thought about it. I know, I know what I want. I want you. I—*cough*—I love you, Maggie."

Then he closed his eyes and his breathing slowed. It was imperceptible, but still extant. Like the white magic, she realized.

She kissed him on the cheek, then limped to the nearest standing stone, ignoring the pain in her shattered foot. She laid her hands on the stone, remembering what she'd seen and heard.

Sarah's assertion: *The white magic is still there... It's just waiting to be pulled out again*

Dougie's explanation: *Deleting something doesn't actually get rid of it... Everything important is still there, invisible, but just waiting to get pulled out again.*

The museum's information: *The stones at Stonehenge were some sort of recording device, preserving in psychic vibration the knowledge of the ancients.*

Maggie looked at her Dark Book, across the grass next to Sarah's limp body. But she didn't need the dark magic any more.

She'd finally found the white magic. She could feel the vibrations in the stone, reverberating into her own bones.

The white magic wanted out.

She let it.

A blinding white light exploded from her stone to the next, connecting them with a wall of white electricity. The energy blasted to the next stone, and the next, lighting each up in a brilliant glow, and sealing her and Iain within the resultant circle of white magic.

She didn't need to think of a spell. It wasn't about words to trick nature; it was about embracing nature and letting it do what it did, only better, faster. She touched her foot and felt the bones knit back together, felt the hole in her flesh close and heal until there wasn't so much as a scar left.

Then she stepped over to Iain. The magic was fairly crackling through her body. The rush from the dark magic was nothing compared to the euphoria consuming her soul as she reached her love.

"*Mo cridhe*," she whispered as she knelt down and laid hands on him. 'My heart.'

Iain's body responded to her touch—in the way it always had, and in ways it never could have. His natural healing power, ordinarily no match for the violence done by two metal slugs tearing through it, accelerated to a frenzied pace. The bullets were pressed through and out of his body, the tissues and organs healing up behind them like a zipper. In a few moments, he was as good as new.

The lightshow dissipated then, until all that was left was an echo of a glow behind each stone, and around the two figures at the center of the circle.

Ellen ran in and up to Philip. She was about to ask what happened, but he silenced her. This wasn't about them.

Iain opened his eyes and looked up at Maggie, his hands searching for the fatal wounds she had removed. Maggie reached down and grabbed his hands. Then she leaned down and kissed him.

When she finally pulled away, she looked him right in those deep blue eyes of his and smiled.

"I love you too."

Epilogue

The 'Tome Tomb' was thriving. Location, location. location, as they say. It found itself at the intersection of trendy and disposable income. Maggie walked into the shop on a sunny November Saturday to find its proprietor attentively straightening the shelves while several customers milled about, looking for books to add to those they'd already selected for purchase.

Sinclair turned when she entered, always the conscientious business owner, and smiled. "Miss Devereaux."

She inclined her head to him. "Mr. Sinclair. Good to see you again." Then, aware that he often knew more than she realized, she added, "I missed you at Callanish."

Sinclair's smile transformed from professional to truly warm. "I was there in spirit."

She nodded and stepped over to the counter. He followed. They were a bit farther away from the customers there. "I don't doubt it," she replied. "Ellen told me you called her. Well, no, actually she said some man called and told her I'd be at the Castle of Park. But the man wouldn't identify himself."

Sinclair grinned and met her gaze. "Then why would I do so now?"

Maggie ignored the question. "How did you know?"

"How did *you* know?" Sinclair turned it back on her.

"I followed the grave robberies," she answered.

Sinclair nodded. And Maggie knew she wasn't the only one who could figure things out.

But that wasn't the most pressing question. "What happened at the Hotel Regency?" she asked.

He nodded again, but the smile gave way to an expression of concern. "You really don't remember, do you?"

Maggie's own smile also faded, into a tight frown. "Apparently I figured out that a certain book needed to be kept away from a certain person until after a certain date. I tried to make myself forget where I'd hidden said book. But I did it a little too well."

Sinclair didn't say anything. He raised an eyebrow to encourage further disclosure.

"I still can't remember anything for several weeks," Maggie admitted. "I was hoping you might fill me in."

At that point, one of the customers came to purchase his selections. There were several and Maggie was glad to see that Sinclair's business seemed to be doing well. When the man had left with his books, Sinclair returned his attention to Maggie.

"You called me," explained. "From the hotel. Honestly, you seemed to be raving a bit. You went on about a prophesy, babies, dark and white magic, and the book we both know you had. You said you needed a place to stay for a few nights. Someplace away from Aberdeen. Someplace where no one would find you. I agreed to reserve a room at the hotel for you. When I arrived, you were unconscious, there was a dead man in the bathtub, and there was no sign of the book you'd finally admitted to."

"So you left me in a hotel room with a dead man?" Maggie

found that less than chivalrous.

"Yes, well…" Sinclair shifted his weight uneasily. "I didn't see a lot of options. There was something about your slumber. It wasn't natural. I tried moving you, but it was as if you were chained to the earth. I was afraid if I moved you, I might injure you somehow. I hardly expected you'd be a suspect in the murder. In fact, as long as you were found unconscious, it would likely appear you were a secondary victim. Hence my call to the police and their speedy arrival. Apparently, however, you woke up a bit too soon."

Maggie shook her head slightly. *Stupid amnesia spell,* she thought. Why couldn't it have knocked her out a few minutes longer?

"So what's next for you, Maggie Devereaux?" Sinclair asked.

A smile crept into the corner of her mouth. "I'm not sure. My criminal case was dismissed, so I won't have to come back to Edinburgh unless I want to. Sarah's criminal case has just started. I expect I'll see her again when I'm called to testify, except that she may be committed to an insane asylum first if she's stupid enough to tell the truth."

"I imagine she may be just that stupid," Sinclair opined.

Maggie had to agree. "And then…" She shrugged, but the rest of her answer walked through the door in the form of a tall, handsome Scotsman.

"Mr. Grant," Sinclair greeted him as he walked in.

Iain stepped over. "Have we met?" he asked genially.

"No," Sinclair answered. He nodded toward Maggie. "But we have a mutual acquaintance."

"Oh, aye," Iain replied. Then he turned to Maggie. "The car's all packed and we're ready to head home. Alex was hoping I could be there this afternoon to go over the books since I left. He never was very good at those."

"Keeping books can be tricky business," Sinclair observed. "But worth the effort."

Maggie smiled. "Aye."

THE END

THE MAGGIE DEVEREAUX PARANORMAL MYSTERIES
Scottish Rite

Blood Rite

Last Rite

THE DAVID BRUNELLE LEGAL THRILLERS
Presumption of Innocence

Tribal Court

By Reason of Insanity

A Prosecutor for the Defense

Substantial Risk

Corpus Delicti

Accomplice Liability

A Lack of Motive

Missing Witness

Diminished Capacity

Devil's Plea Bargain

Homicide in Berlin

Premeditated Intent

Alibi Defense

THE TALON WINTER LEGAL THRILLERS
Winter's Law

Winter's Chance

Winter's Reason

Winter's Justice

Winter's Duty

Winter's Passion

ALSO BY STEPHEN PENNER
The Godling Club

Mars Station Alpha

ABOUT THE AUTHOR

Stephen Penner is an author, artist, and attorney from Seattle.

In addition to writing the Maggie Devereaux Paranormal Mysteries, he is also the author of the David Brunelle Legal Thriller Series, featuring Seattle homicide prosecutor David Brunelle; the Talon Winter Legal Thrillers, starring Tacoma criminal defense attorney Talon Winter; and several stand-alone works.

For more information, please visit *www.stephenpenner.com*.